Within the
Space of the
Moment

Within the Space of the Moment

Espen Vidar

TURNING
STONE
PRESS

First published in 2012 by Turning Stone Press, an imprint of
Red Wheel/Weiser, LLC

With offices at:
665 Third Street, Suite 400
San Francisco, CA 94107
www.redwheelweiser.com

ISBN (paperback): 978-1-61852-019-7

ISBN (hardcover): 978-1-61852-018-0

Cover design by Jim Warner

Printed in the United States of America

IBT

10 9 8 7 6 5 4 3 2 1

Truth belongs to no one and everyone.

Contents

Stones in the Pockets   1

Know Thyself   5

A Friendly Game of Zennis   25

Face Your Fear   41

The Power of Presence   53

The Thirsty Few   67

Limitations of Mind   79

Enlightenment How?   93

Contemplation of the Six Elements   105

Spiritual Arrogance   119

Seeds No More   139

Water in Motion   145

Stones in the Pockets

I woke up reluctantly, with an agonizing hangover, in the dunes on Arambol Beach, Goa, India. It was the year 2000. The apocalypse was still absent and the millennium celebration had lasted me four continuous months. A more enlightened soul would have enjoyed the sunrise, but I was strangely hot and wet on the right leg. That's solely why I woke and looked around. With lifted leg, a wild dog, full of fleas for sure, was pissing on me. I kicked, missed, and it snapped. And somewhere in the back of my mind lyrics played compulsively, like a runaway jukebox. This time it was echoing from Pink Floyd's "Dark Side of the Moon": *I've always been mad, I know I've been mad, like the most of us.* No drink, no drug, no combination of the two could switch it off. I possessed a ruthless habit of having an unstoppable noise, in the mixed form of inner dialogue and music-poetry, running around in my brain. Without getting up, I managed to hit the rabies bastard on the nose. It disappeared, whimpering, and my eyes slipped. *Is there anybody out there?*

Noise in the fog. Local fishermen came to shore. Their night catch must have been rewarding, as, smiling, they were pushing their boats loudly onto the beach. They, these others, were satisfied with so little, and I dissatisfied with so much. I remained lying down—down the drain—it was a self-torturing time to take stock, but my mind was mercilessly rewinding the tape. Once again I scanned the film of my life. No children—luckily, I had made sure of that. Relationships—many, and one divorce—peak beginnings and then unhappily ever after. Three interrupted careers. Goals reached and goals lost. And so what? Once, I had been such a promising young man from the land of the midnight sun. And now, my current status: a fugitive, an economic criminal on the run, with periodic suffering from recurrent depressions.

Incomprehensibly enough, most people whom I met seemed to like me. I was thirty-nine years old and it seemed like I had already tried most alternatives, most avenues of existence, with no lasting happiness or satisfaction whatsoever: materially, mentally, emotionally, experientially. I felt pleasure less and less, misery more and more. Hopelessness or despair, more precisely. A vibrating void. Not even the local mixtures of alcohol, Ecstasy, and amphetamine—and the Goa trance dance—dulled the incurable pain. Only one untested alternative was left, and I knew how.

Simon Mollat's final solution: After dark, I would sneak down and borrow a small fishing boat. The black and green one by the river's mouth would be perfect. I would fill my pockets with stones and dive downward as far as my lungs would allow me. Away from suffering. Too far for any return. Toward the deep blue . . .

Something intervened, took me out of the mental maelstrom, and got my attention. Something against my chest. An itch. A joker had shoved a paper ball in the neck opening of my T-shirt. Irritated, I unfolded the paper. A black and white picture of an old, wrinkled Indian met my eyes, a flyer. About the small letters I didn't bother. I read the title only: **Freedom from this "me"**. Signed, a somebody called **Raman Kavalam**. *Ha! Chanting my way to divinity with an Indian guru? Hardly. It smelled like incense, like the esoteric sixties, with sects, robes, and brainwashing.* Again my eyes slipped.

The sun was already in Zenith when I eventually got up on my feet. It was surprisingly hard to make it up to standing. Somehow all of the pockets in my vest and pants were already filled with stones. The extra weight made me sway. I gazed at the ocean's infinity. Took one step with shaking legs, stopped, and had one of those unpleasant moments of knowing nothing. *Where am I? Why? What has happened?* In a rush of fright I looked down and gazed at the only focal point in the sand. At the flyer and at its cryptic title. **Freedom from this "me"?**

Come to think of it, not one, but two untested alternatives were left . . . one tiny problem with the latter only. I didn't believe in God.

"Are you truly up for it? Challenging your own ego-identity? Or are you just another honey-thief?"

Know Thyself

Circles evaporating in water. Plop, plop. A ritualized goodbye. I don't know why, or how even, but I did it: I dropped all my drugs in the Indian Ocean, left the party scene in Goa, and now bumped along with heavy thoughts sinking like stones, a good day's bus journey south to the coastal town of Alappuzha in Kerela. To a wet greenhouse world of fluorescent emerald color.

Full of anxiety, I found myself sitting in the living room of former Air India pilot Raman Kavalam, known to an intimate few as Captain Ram. Some basic information about this mystic figure had come my way. He was considered the last purist, in the sense that he insisted on direct transmission and therefore allowed no cameras. In fact, it was said that if he had used the Internet he might have become the biggest name on the contemporary spiritual scene. His comment was simply that in true spirituality, quantity was compromising quality. "The teacher's teacher," as he was called, used to hold *Satsangs*, or meetings in Truth, in a former cinema hall in New Delhi.

At the age of eighty-six and recently diagnosed with terminal cancer, Raman had now moved back to his birth home in Alappuzha. Having taken what was called a Bodhisattva vow, though, promising to share the Truth "till my last breath," he was still holding Satsang an hour or two every Friday evening, against medical advice. According to rumors, Raman was in chronic pain, but nobody could really tell for sure from his appearance.

As it was the month of May and the beginning of the rainy season, only his closest devotees and a few passersby were gathered in the old-fashioned room. Approximately fifteen people were sitting in two rows and a half circle of living room furniture around Raman's wheelchair and his guest chair, now occupied by a debating philosophy professor from Jaipur. Their debate was filled with abstractions and was way over my head.

The only thing I understood was that the cocky professor was not there to understand or to learn, but simply to win, and as I waited my turn, I found myself going back some thirty years in memory. To the twenty-first of July 1969, a little after three in the morning exactly. I was awakened by my father's whiskey breath, just in time to see in our black and white television set a ghost, or more precisely, Neil Armstrong, putting his left foot on the moon. "... *one small step for man, one giant leap for mankind.*" My father lifted me up, was ecstatic. "What exciting times to grow up, kiddo! Soon, all is known.

All secrets revealed. For your generation, everything is possible!"

My uncle, who was the wise one in the family and also drunk, and who two years later killed himself driving off a cliff, caught me and sat me down as he exclaimed, "All is soon known about the outside, son, but do not be fooled. About the inside secrets, the soul, man knows next to nothing. Above the gates of the Oracle in Delphi was, for a reason, written 'Know thyself,' and that, Simon, is what you should ask yourself growing up: 'Who is this *me*?'"

The professor had started out self-assured and offensive, but obviously defeated by the reappearing word "consciousness," he now seemed close to a speechless knockout. To the audience's apparent satisfaction, he just stood up and left. *Is that the game? Meet our guru and he will prove you wrong? King of the Hill? Isn't that some kind of an ego game?* I felt myself as if in the wrong place and as if a little devil inside had already decided to smoke a fat joint and leave with the Hampi bus the same night. But I hadn't come this far for nothing, so I waved my arm.

Raman met my eyes with a gaze like an ocean of stillness reflected. A look that triggered something inside of me, for sure, a lurking fright? Fortunately it didn't stop my mouth from speaking what I had silently rehearsed. "Raman, sir, I have come all the way from Norway. Please tell me the truth, with words on my own level, no abstractions, no all this that I have just been hearing, no Absolute and Relative truth, no Manifest and Un-manifest or Dualistic or Non-dualistic. Simply, only. This question has followed me all my life: 'Who is this *me*?' By the way, I am Simon Mollat."

The old man smiled with a face full of lines and wrinkles. His voice was soft.

" 'I am' is correct. 'Simon Mollat' is wrong."

I looked at him, confused. He waved me forward with his walking cane. I sat down in the disreputable operation-chair as he chuckled, addressing the rest of the meeting." 'I am.' I'll get back to that . . ."

Well seated, I met his eyes once again, up close this time, and I literally grabbed the arms of the chair so as not to drown in them. There was an almost hypnotic depth in this old captain's eyes, a force and a clarity that completely overshadowed the fact that his wrinkled skin was yellow from jaundice."Sir, I don't even believe in God . . ."

"Yes, 'God' is such a polluted word, isn't it? For communication purposes, so imprecise. It indicates a multitude of different things to different people. Like one sound's different meanings in one hundred languages. And believing has no purpose, really, has it? Belief as such only hinders true understanding and is a poor substitute for reality. We hold beliefs concerning things we don't know about from direct experience simply because mentally we can't stand to stay in the not-knowing. And like this, developing complex systems of beliefs, we become more interested in defending them than in knowing what is true. What-is thus becomes secondary to shielding what-I-believe-to-be."

I looked at him in amazement. Despite both age and illness, his arms and torso were surprisingly full of gestures and intensity. "So in your teaching there is no need to believe in God?"

"No need for beliefs in anything, really. But then also not to forget, Simon: The other mental polarity, 'non-believing,' can easily be transformed into a blocked conviction in your mind, as strong as anything. Mine is a scientific approach, neither believing nor non-believing. All preconceptions prevent our possibilities of—in a spiritual sense and in the course of true inquiry—knowing, or realizing, what . . . what your conditioned mind very well may be trying to avoid, what truly is. In my experience it is only the advanced and confident, the conscious, who have the open courage to question their own sets of beliefs. You see, Simon, for most people, saying these three words can be mentally devastating: *I don't know.* So do you? Know?"

What is he getting at? Know what? I already felt slow. Like a turtle, with Raman's words hammering on my shell. "What I think . . ."

"Yes, thinking thoughts, one after another, an unstoppable stream, isn't it? And on the contrary to what you may think, Simon, be aware that it's not so much you who control your thoughts, as it is your thoughts which control you."

For a tiny moment I was stopped in my tracks. "But . . ." Raman chuckled and measured me, as if considering what dance step would do the trick. "Don't worry. We will take care of your 'but list,' step by step. First, let's talk seriously about the issue you have raised, a very essential one, about introspection, Self-knowledge."

"Who is this 'me'?"

"Yes. There are, in general, two ways to go about it. Initially: If you don't truly know who you are, how can you be sure what you want in life? Now, the propaganda from governments, corporations, and media all makes us assume that wanting more, or different, or better, always being hungry for the next thing, is the way to live—a desirable condition. From a position of vested interests, they are fueling a feeling of lack and are convincing masses of people to go on a lifelong ride of discontentment, an addictive carousel-trip of consumption—money, status, relationships, things—that does not lead anyone to lasting happiness or fulfillment. All this, even though science periodically reveals to us that this chasing for 'more in the future' doesn't really lead to durable contentment for anybody, that it's a lie."

"A lie?"

"Absolutely. Outer pleasures simply don't bring lasting joy. In best cases, only relative comfort. And any short-term gratification gained doesn't heal our longing for permanent happiness. A recent research study concluded that if two twins, with a similar basic level of happiness, on the same morning respectively won big in the lottery and were injured in a car accident, one year later they would both be back more or less on the same equal level of happiness as before the drama occurred! Rather, it seems, as the advertising business is well aware of, that the more we get, the more we feel we need. Hence, it has been said that trying to find lasting happiness from better relationships and more possessions is like drinking salt water to quench your thirst. The main point being that when all basic needs are covered—with the deepest respect for those who struggle with poverty—outer circumstances only have a transient effect on our happiness level. Despite this scientific fact, only a minority of individuals during their lifespan see through this deceitful cobweb of 'outer-more' which forms their life . . . You follow my drift, Simon?"

Drinking salt water . . . a metaphor, I had to admit, *not without a brackish resonance.* I sneezed, and Raman proceeded. "Seeing through the cobweb, as I said, and if they don't resign or remain unaware of the alternative, they naturally turn their aim of fulfillment away from the world of manifestations. A seemingly never-ending outer happiness-search, finally, in some unique human entities doing a 180-degree U-turn and pointing them within. Toward an inward journey. A courageous minority, really, breaking free from society's thousands of years of conditioning, following a deeper feeling that there has to be more to existence than just mental and physical objects. That a basis for happiness, then, or contentment, or fulfillment, is to be sought within yourself—in the non-material."

My uncle's words in a new dressing? "You make it sound easy and appealing. Yet this minority, as you call them, they are still operating with no guarantee of happiness-success, aren't they? Because maybe lasting happiness, or contentment, just isn't humanly possible?" I waved my arms. "Maybe this, this shadow-life, so to speak, just is all that destiny has in store for most of us?"

"Maybe. Maybe also why Plato suggested that most people see the world as if imprisoned in a dark cave, looking at the shadows on the wall and believing that they are real."

"Had Plato found the key to lasting happiness, then?"

"Good question, Simon. And about this key, exactly: Isn't it *maybe* a fact that fearing or needing nothing, a mind utterly in peace, is the only true foundation for happiness to flower?"

Inner peace equals happiness? A perspective that had never occurred to me. *Very simple. Too simple.* I doubted, as I did with most new perspectives, and Raman smiled at my facial expression. "The question then being: What does it mean, in light of all this, getting to know oneself? Who are you, Simon?"

"Besides my name, age, and body, I guess . . . a loser."

"Peter?" Raman nodded toward a young Englishman sitting on the front bench, who smiled: "Only losers can win in this game."

"How is that, Peter?"

"Through disillusionment."

"Through the force of disillusionment, yes. A force which *may* evoke a crucial change. Simon, are you still with us?"

I was just about to space out in my own compulsive thoughts. I compensated by talking too much and too loudly. "Losing and winning what, exactly? What game are we talking about? How to play your lousy cards dealt in life, is that it? As if you have a choice, really? So about this disillusionment, there is a huge resonance, yes. But absolutely not as a winning force?"

Raman smiled. "It seems, Simon, that first when the illusion of happiness or fulfillment found in an outer chase loses its fairy-tale grip, a deeper dissatisfaction occurs. A force necessary to make some of us in its place search within for something which we really don't know, something that is 'higher.' So the society-appointed 'winner' then stays in the old game, bound to be discontent sooner or later, and the 'loser' may break free to a whole new arena."

"Okay . . ."

"And your word—'loser'—is, by the way, just another label of the surface of identity enjoyed by your self-judging superego. A false sense of self. Just because your favorite color is blue and you like jam better than honey doesn't mean you know yourself, Simon. Knowing oneself, in your understanding to begin with, on the personality level, more than anything, means watching one's reactions in everyday relationship to people, things, concepts, and one's own emotions. To in this way know one's patterns in relationship reactions, especially where conflicts occur."

For a moment, I lost myself in memories. Conflicting scenes from the breakup of my marriage came to mind. If that was who I was, I didn't like it. *It is not who I want to be.* Raman's ongoing voice brought me back. "Telling yourself the truth is alpha and omega. The willingness at any moment to stop and ask yourself: 'What is going on?' What is going on, Simon?"

Going on? Puzzled, I heard myself reply. "I am doing my best, sir."

"And that is all you can do at any given moment, isn't it? So just relax, and don't worry about a thing. We are still only scratching the surface of 'this me,' Simon, and our friendly investigation must not be confused with any sort of Self-improvement. Nothing wrong in wanting to improve oneself. But Self-improvement, which often becomes a never-ending process, may become a disturbance in the overall introspection. It takes you out of the present. Away from being. What-is is avoided by future-projecting ideas of what-should-be. Hence, most people don't want to wake up from their mental self-hypnosis; they just want a sweeter dream! And the window out of all this, the opening to peace, joy, and divinity is . . . ?"

A smiling old Indian woman answered, "Being within the space of the moment."

I must have looked like a question mark, because there was laughter in the room: friendly laughter, but laughter all the same.

Raman just ignored it and nodded. "Fine words, yet words are just concepts, indicators, pointers to the truth, not the truth itself. Bubbles, merely, in the ocean of consciousness. Are you with me so far, Simon? Do you understand the essence of what I am conveying?"

Nothing I thought I knew beforehand seemed to hold any weight here. Even so, I didn't feel threatened in any way. Being with this old Indian was kind of an overflowing experience, like turning on a mystery tap. "In small glimpses."

Raman smiled. "Small glimpses are better than total darkness."

I smiled back tentatively, bravely.

"You see, Simon, most people are afraid to truly look at themselves beyond the superficial level, because they fear they may not like what they will find. When you don't know who you are—and believe me, hardly anybody does—you create a mind-made self as a substitute. Protecting that false sense of self—your mask or persona—then becomes your primary motivating force."

A false face? That surely didn't apply to me. To my father, now and then, yes. And to some of my friends, maybe. *What's wrong with having a personality, anyway? What exactly does this old Indian want? A world of feature-less people?*

"Be aware, Simon, because your ego is in protection as we speak. It constantly re-creates itself for its mistaken identity to uphold."

"And what is the problem with that, then?"

Raman gave me a fierce look. "It is *the* problem! The purpose of life, for far too many, becomes an unconscious intensifying of the fiction of 'me.' And a corresponding daily amplifying of the voice or dialogue in their head. I, me, mine, and what's next. Confirming 'me and my story.'"

"But this is normal . . ."

Raman smiled sadly. "The problem with this kind of 'normality,' Simon, this internal storytelling, is as if you have built your house on sand, you have to spend most of your energy to keep the walls standing. Even among seekers of truth, the not so unusual way is deceit and escape rather than truthfulness, rather than a sweet little pain when self-deception is revealed. So honestly, Simon, I ask you, does any of this ring a little true to you, maybe?"

Reluctantly processing under the surgeon's inquiring glance, I wondered, *Isn't there a mental construct within the myriad of thoughts, a me-story I may be unconsciously, and even obsessively, upholding?* "I can see the tip of something, I am sorry to say, yes."

"Don't be sorry; it's true for everybody. Rather, be happy for telling yourself the truth and through this insight maybe learning what you are not, thereby being left with an understanding closer to what is your authentic Self. Because just as the eye cannot see itself, neither can the ego-mind, the persona or the 'me.' So the question that finally arises must be who, or what is it that sees or witnesses that which you are not, your false self, the story of 'me'?"

Overload digesting. This advanced psychology was like being able to see oneself from the outside, so to speak: observing, not being, one's thoughts. It was as if the gears in my never-resting brain were slipping. Yet in a few glimpses of reluctant clarity I was seeing some of the mechanisms within me that he was describing: the unstoppable voice in my head and its patterns of identity-upholding and storytelling. More importantly, being in his company, I was now surprisingly feeling some of my heaviness lifting. The weight of anxiety. "But isn't this kind of an egoistic journey, sir, being so focused on oneself?"

"On the contrary. It is liberation from the ego-grip. A conscious life is no longer burdening your environment with your false self, with your unfinished business, spreading selfless joy, peace, and love rather than operating from an ego-agenda."

"Okay . . ."

" 'Till the false is seen as the false, truth is not, right, Simon?"

"Sounds true."

Raman chuckled. "At a certain point in anybody's life, it is essential to take some time and, metaphorically, like the young Buddha, Prince Siddhartha, leave family and palace behind and head for the forest. Some time to de-identify with all the social roles that are being played without and within: as a son, father, brother, friend, colleague, lover, or husband. Some time to renounce the group, for true Self-knowledge to bloom."

"It sounds a bit lonely and painful."

"No buds burst without pain."

"Again true."

Raman smiled once again. "You know, Simon, I wasn't always a spiritual teacher. I have had a long life with many mundane experiences. Some sixty years ago, before my career as a pilot, I had long periods of feeling lost. In fact, I became a compulsive gambler: horses, dice, you name it, in a futile attempt to get some spark back into my meaningless life. To keep it short, I lost all my money, and my father's with it. But the good thing, in retrospect, was that my arrogant, self-protective ego was humbled. This first crack in the programmed mind-shell later made it possible for some light to enter. As we are talking, I sense something similar in you, and I want you to know its value. Only from a humiliation like this, and a consequential humbleness, can Self-realization happen. Which means knowing who you are beyond the surface self: beyond your name, your body, your roles, and story. But don't take my word for any of this. Investigate for yourself. The question then remains, Simon: Are you truly up for it? Challenging your own ego-identity? Or are you just another honey-thief?"

Although I was aware that I didn't fully grasp the meaning of more than perhaps half of what the old man was saying, it all struck me as somewhat persuasive on a higher level. As a suddenly revealed way out, even, of my basement darkness, a ray of hope. I looked around me. It seemed like everybody was looking supportively back. A few good-looking girls, even; I didn't care. *Honey-thief?* It felt like an accusation, and it brought a sense of the displaced life, shame, as one of my darkest moments appeared before me in a flashback. Humbled me more than any. I pushed it aside. Solemnly I straightened my back in an inexplicable impulse to expose. "Raman, sir, honestly, I have been on the extremes. Have spent many long months on the dark side of the moon, been far out on the crazy side, even, so I guess I don't have so much invested in my ego-identity anymore."

Raman's eyes sparkled. "So can a madman become a sage, a Buddha? That would be turning failure into success, wouldn't it? A crashed life producing a flower? Yes, as the lotus is rooted in mud, it has been suggested more than once that a madman, more than anyone, can become a Buddha. Fully experiencing the madness of mind, its hold on you may get a liberating crack. No longer, then, clinging to a futile hope of finding lasting happiness or permanent fulfillment in any confirmations of a story. And also because the final Truth, the shift into the unknown freedom, in perception is so beyond your mental constructions that even a taste of it scares many average neurotics back to so-called normality. Very good, Simon. No depth in the painting without a little black on the palette."

Buddha, lotus, depth, and a little black on the palette. Such reassurance! Words worth saving, really, in the depths of my soul. If only I could believe in them.

Raman gave me another warm smile. "Only when unconsciousness like greed, lust, ambition, judgments, and fear do not get the best of us and we are true to ourselves do we live in a peace not dependent on the situation. So back to you, then, and your 'me,' and the now-dawning seeing: seeing through the strategies of the ego. Analyzing your programming: your genes plus your conditioning. It may be a lifelong project, you know. A way of living life, of being . . ."

Lifelong!? From the expression in his eyes, I couldn't tell if he was joking or dead serious. "You initially said 'two ways to go about it,' the other being . . . ?"

"Self-inquiry. More direct, more of a confrontational shortcut. But nothing for honey-thieves. You are interested?"

"Yes."

Peter, the front-bencher, let out a sound of recognition, and Raman smiled. "I will give you some homework, then. Ask yourself all the way through, you may even write down all the answers: *'Who am I?'* Or, in your case, better, I feel: *'Who is this me?'* And when you eventually lean back—say, after a week of intense inquiry—with a bunch of 'I, me, mine' answers—and you still maybe feel that this bundle of thoughts is not covering who you are, then ask, Simon: *'Who sees this? Who is observing, witnessing this story-material?'* Or even more precisely, ask yourself: *'To whom do these thoughts appear?'* And whatever label you give the answer: At the core, that's exactly who you are! Consciousness itself. Awareness. The sense of presence. Existing-ness, if you like. *I am.*"

"I am?"

"Yes. I am: Not this or that, just I know *I am.* Also to be understood as pure *beingness.* Some may use the more abstract term *soul*; others the more poetic term *heart of hearts.* I prefer consciousness, and I verbalize this in so many ways as I find relevant words and concepts, Simon, because spirituality is all about *who* you experience yourself to be. The ego-mind or consciousness. The deceiver or the perceiver. The tiny cloud or the whole sky. You will find that you have so much less to defend as you come to know yourself as bigger than your story. The activities of thought experienced as a witness, rather than the hypnotic composition of who you are. Do you feel or follow what I am pointing at?"

"I am . . ."

Raman chuckled. "Good, but please don't make this another mental layer in your mind, a learned concept, another object of thought that needs my operational removal! Knowing doesn't do it. You have to realize this, this *I am*, for yourself, Simon, for a deeper understanding to happen. Lao Tzu, the founder of Tao, wrote some twenty-six hundred years ago: 'The one who knows himself is enlightened.' And I add: Know your Self and you know everybody."

"I am not looking for enli—"

He didn't let me finish. "Yes, yes. I expect a report next week from you. You will come?"

Again I looked around the room. Nothing but supportive eyes looked back at me. Loving gazes, even. *What is the catch? Does it matter?* I turned my eyes toward Raman again and my doubt momentarily vanished. Graspable or not, it was as if the essence of what was said was already known somewhere within me. "I will come."

"Enough for today, then. Okay, Peter?"

"Okay, Raman."

"Ah! So may I be right in assuming then that you are searching freedom from a never-ending voice in your head, from mental movie-making and self-created suffering?"

A Friendly Game of Zennis

Everybody was sitting with their eyes closed, contemplating to the live sitar music. Fourteen participants this Friday evening, half of whom were Indians, half Europeans, plus the sitar player and Raman and his nurse. And me. I peeped in childish secrecy. Men and women, from their early twenties to maybe sixty years old; with closed eyes they all seemed so peaceful, as if they had something and I didn't. *'Cause I try and I try and I try and I try. I can't get no, I can't get no, I can't get no satisfaction.* Peter probably didn't listen to the Rolling Stones. The serene front-bencher whom Raman approached last Satsang, one week ago, had taken pity on me during the past week and tried to teach me *Zazen*, a traditional sitting meditation, supposedly practiced for one hour every morning. But my mind was so active, or busy, or disturbed, even, I was sure that the peace and rest that was meant to occur was light-years away.

Seven sober and tedious days it had been. In Alappuzha's backwater. I had checked the bus departures several times. Hampi, Varanasi, or Mumbai? Booked a ticket once, even. I wanted to leave, but I didn't. I stayed, waiting. *Waiting for what, exactly? For more long hours of fruitless self-scrutiny? Who is this me? Why would a sworn atheist expose himself to one week of self-torment for two hours sitting with a spiritual teacher?* It made no sense.

Yet my second Satsang had come, and only the word held some kind of indefinable gravitas. I read *Zen and the Art of Motorcycle Maintenance* as a teenager in the late seventies, and I had an aha! experience when Bjørn Borg said in a victory interview given almost at that same time that "A tennis game consists of only one ball, the one that is at play." This memory pretty much summed up my insight into this assumed kind of spirituality, a spirituality outside all belief systems, an exploring of the divine force within, or however they liked to name their castle in the air.

Finally the sitar music stopped. Raman opened his eyes and looked for a few seconds at each one of us. A new participant, a striking young woman with an impressive bronze-colored curly crop of hair, raised her arm and was the first to get his verbal attention.

"Yes?"

"Raman, sir, my name is Silvia. My teacher, your old student, Suresha, in Tel Aviv, in a way has sent me here."

Raman smiled. "Suresha. How is she?"

"She is fine, sir. She does Satsang twice a week, often with more than fifty attendants, and she quotes you in almost every meeting. It was the will of the source for me to at last be in your presence and for my finalization to happen here."

Raman paused. "You are most welcome here, Silvia. And when the opportunity presents itself, send my love to Suresha. But about your 'finalization,' we don't know, do we?"

"I am ripe, sir."

"Yes, yet at the end of the day we all humbly have to accept the state of being that grace has in store for us, don't we? Satsang, being in association with Truth or consciousness, is no school or university with an accumulation of knowledge and a final passing exam. Even in a supportive group like this, and with me as your guide and inspiration, there still is no guarantee for—let's label it for the occasion—a permanent change in perspective to occur."

"I know . . ."

"Self-realization cannot be achieved, nor can it be given. Nevertheless, given the right internal circumstances and a mysterious grace, a discovery, or recognition, can . . . just happen."

Corrected, Silvia lowered her eyes and remained silent. I sensed an opening, gathered courage, and waved my arm. I was for the second week in a row invited up into the hot seat by Raman's side. For maybe a minute he was just looking at me, tuning himself into my soul-like vibrations or something before he broke the silence. "So you made it to Satsang, Simon. I am happy to see you again. And about your Self-inquiry? What is your report?"

"Raman, sir, inquiring into myself, repeatedly asking 'Who is this me?' I get maybe thirty-something replies, a bunch of answers where even the sum of these fragments remains unsatisfactory, and a reinforced feeling that I am not merely my name, body, and relations, my past, or my projected future."

"Good."

"Yes, but this being 'I am' or consciousness, or maybe a soul, even . . . Well, I tried, I really did, but honestly, it feels like an abstraction. However I looked, one way or the other, I found myself to be made up of somewhat the same. It is always a 'me'! So I guess I will need your further guidance, maybe . . . to get to this other identity-side?"

Raman seemed to enjoy himself. "A Zen story, first: One day a young seeker of truth on his journey home came to the banks of a wide river. Staring hopelessly at the great obstacle in front of him, he pondered for hours on just how to cross such a wide barrier. Just as he was about to give up his pursuit to continue his journey, he saw a well-known teacher on the other side of the river. The young seeker yelled over to the teacher, 'Oh wise one, can you tell me how to get to the other side?' The teacher looked up and down the river, paused for a short moment, and yelled convincingly back, 'My son, you are on the other side . . .'"

I stared at him. Once again drowning in the old man's eyes.

"So, Simon, I will return to your inquiry, but first, tell me: You are approximately halfway through life. With the remains of your days, what do you want?"

You are on the other side. I didn't really hear the question, spaced out for a split second. And now, being somehow welcomed as an insider, as I understood it, I was suddenly eager to show him that I knew something. So I threw a ball up in the air and served. "I like Zen."

"You like Zen?"

"Yes, when I was a teenager I considered Bjørn Borg my Zen master."

"The tennis player?"

"A man of the moment, a one-ball-at-a-time kind of guy."

"A Zen master in the underwear business?" Raman laughed, and everybody in the living room laughed with him. I managed to put up a smile, having a creeping feeling that I, or my ego, as I had now learned to discriminate, was in trouble. He kept chuckling. "When thoughts fall away, Simon, laughter starts. Some chai?"

Raman lifted a teapot to underline the seemingly innocent question. I nodded, surprised. He poured milk-tea, and kept pouring as the chai overflooded from my cup. After a few seconds I couldn't help myself. "Sir. It is overfull." Everybody laughed again. Raman kept pouring as he quoted someone: "Like this cup, you are full of your own opinions and speculations. How can I show you Zen unless you first empty your cup?"

Raman smiled together with his audience and put the chai pot down. "The Japanese master Nan-in." Suddenly he changed to a serious face again. "Zen, Sufi, Tao, Tantra, Advaita, Vipassana, Chi Qong, Yoga, Tai Chi . . . they are all means to the same end. What do you really want, Simon? That is the question. It is next to impossible to be of any support when you come to me, in the middle of your life, and you don't even know what you want. Tell me, and we shall see if I can be of any assistance."

"I am thinking about it, sir. Real hard."

"Thinking, according to your preference, Zen, is more the problem, not the solution. You have to be seeking something, otherwise you would rather be on the beach looking at bikinis right now, wouldn't you?"

"Bikinis somehow have dropped out of my list, sir, but there was a kind of immediate resonance happening, I was triggered by reading the title of your pamphlet: *Freedom from this 'me.'*"

"Ah! So may I be right in assuming, then, that you are searching freedom from a never-ending voice in your head, from mental movie-making and self-created suffering?"

I looked astonished at him. "I guess so . . ."

"When the dervish whirls, when the yogi chants, when any artist pursues her flow, and when European youngsters take Ecstasy in Goa and dance all night at raves, they are all deep down, like you, seeking freedom from this 'me,' are they not?"

"I haven't given it all that much thought, really."

"And so what would it give you?"

"What?"

Raman gave me an overpowering look. "If the negative, suffering, is removed, what's the positive that remains?"

I fumbled. "I don't know, something I had in my long-lost childhood, I guess, joy, maybe . . . and some kind of peace within."

"Peace and joy . . . Very good indeed, Simon! And in realizing *that,* I may be of some assistance. Let's start the operational preparations with how Zen may approach existence for the essence of Self, for peace in mind and joy of being, to happen. Okay, Simon? Is your cup empty?" His eyes looked straight through me.

I took a deep breath. Caught off guard, I tried to check within. "As empty as I know how, sir."

Raman smiled a dry smile. "Then that will do. For now. Zen essential number one: A man has the crucial choice of living his life either as a 'no' or as a 'yes' to the present moment. 'No' is nourishment for the basis of his suffering— the ego—and it is war against life, as such, which forever takes place in the here-now war against existence. 'Yes,' on the other hand, weakens the ego-grip. It means opening your doors and windows to that-which-is. In fact, whenever you deeply accept this moment as it is, within you and without—no matter what forms it takes and without labeling it—you are still, you are at peace. So it may happen that walking out of a disliked situation is the best response to what-is, but often, like in work, for instance, that is not an option. So I repeat: When you say 'yes' to the isness of life, when you truly accept this moment as it is, you can feel a loosening of the 'knot,' a softening around the mind-contraction, a sense of spaciousness within you that is deeply peaceful."

Raman looked at me and I couldn't help looking down. Trying to grasp the consequences of what was being said, it again sounded all too simple. "Yes?" *Like a magic formula? Whatever is, could not be otherwise? And spaciousness? Another abstract.* In respect, I tried to camouflage my skepticism, knowing that I hardly could hide anything from this powerful set of measuring eyes.

Raman smiled at me. "Out of this sprouts another Zen trait: a nonreactive relationship to all experiences. A responsibility, really, in the more precise meaning of the word: an ability to respond. Either spontaneously from intuition and the gut feeling, or sincerely from consciousness itself, rather than mechanically from the roam of thoughts and emotions."

An ability to respond? Fancy formulation. I wasn't aware that my eyes were wandering.

"I can sense your resistance, Simon, and at this stage, it is quite natural. However, are you all set for surgery, part one? It is just a small cut in your mentality, really, a tiny reprogramming in your software, with no need for anaesthetization."

The room temperature instantly changed from warm to cold. A rush of fright. My brainwashing fear was triggered. In less than a moment I was ready to get up and leave the room. Then he bubbled reassuringly over with laughter. The whole room cracked open in laughter with him. A laughter *with* me, rather than *at* me. And as if Raman read my mind, he said: "I will not shape you into something you are not or that you don't want to be. I play my part as a teacher sincerely. The root meaning of the Latin word *educare* is 'to bring out that which is within,' and I see my role in this chair solely as that of a midwife revealing in the student that which is already there. What is already in you, Simon!"

"Okay."

"Okay? And you sitting there and me sitting here, it is just roles we engage in in the play of life, not meaning your worth or mine is any different. And let it also be clear that all my past, and all your past, has brought us to this moment, that—looking back—this moment as it manifests here couldn't really have been any different, and every other possibility, you not being here for instance, is just mental masturbation, isn't it? So if you, without too much mental resistance, can accept a simple fact like this with me, then repeat: *The present moment is as it is, always.*"

I took a deep breath. "The present moment is as it is, always . . ."

Raman nodded. "It gives your mind an opportunity for some much-needed rest, doesn't it? A free base, really. And apropos mental relaxation and a corresponding spaciousness, know that in Zen, *presence*, or wakefulness, is the name of the game. You see, most people have such a small layer of presence—let's say maybe twenty percent—but a man of a still mind is one hundred percent present. You can feel his presence from the outside, as a charisma. His being is a radiation of a silent state within. So the 'trance'—or let us call it the degree of identification with mind—differs from person to person. Some people enjoy periods of freedom from it, however brief, and the peace, joy, and aliveness they experience in those moments make life worth living. These are also the moments in a life when creativity, love, and compassion arise. Others, though, are sadly and constantly spellbound in a narrow mind-state that needs constant fixing and confirmation. Ensnared as they are in the false belief that their story, their mind-voice, is all that they are, trapped like this by mental turmoil, restlessness, and suffering, they are hardly present in any situation."

Eighty percent absence, a sleep-walking humanity, myself included? I tried to look back at some of my life.

My memory blurred. *Was this why? My relationships, had they mostly been experienced as if in a trance? My last marriage, for instance, with Anna, at breakfast, dinner, and even during lovemaking, I saw her sensual face under me. Had I unconsciously been carrying a filter between me and her? Been under some kind of a spell? In a stream of thought-hypnosis: mentally four-fifths somewhere else? The only full exception, maybe, during and after orgasm?* I took a deep breath and moistened my lips. Even though the "buts" were lining up in the back of my mind, I managed to resist the impulse to initiate a provoked debate. I responded, probably, rather than reacted. "The present moment is as it is, always."

Again this flash of a smile to which I could easily become addicted. As I now had been led to understand, I could feel Raman's charismatic presence and how it transmuted to me.

"Good. Now, interrelated, Zen essential number two . . ."

"Yes?"

"*To live in the present is the only way to live.* With no past dragging you backward and no future pulling you forward. No more indulgence in has-been and should-be. The shape of this moment is the golden gate out of the fictional story of 'me,' is your access to consciousness, to spirit, and the divine."

"To live in the present, simply . . ."

"It is obvious, isn't it? Isn't it a fact that all experience takes place in the present? And that apart from this experience, nothing really exists? So whenever your mind starts moving somewhere away from this reality, bring it gently back here. When it starts moving to the past, to the future, bring it lovingly to the now. Many a student before you has changed their habit of mind and their level of presence in this way. Continuously returning their attention to the timeless present moment, to a point of still mind, rather than to be repetitively caught up in past-future-absence and mental movie-making."

I did an interior check just to find my mind wandering horizontally—past, present, future—nonstop. Awareness thereof, occasionally. Focus, attention. Trying, bringing it to the moment. Too much effort.

Raman read my mind once more. "Eventually, through practice, it will be effortless. And don't forget—let this be surgery, part two—that the moment is more vast than any content that arises in it. The present is what-is, is unchanging consciousness, is the space in which manifestations happen, mental as well as physical. A space-awareness like this in the outer exactly, to give you something to strive for, stimulates a spaciousness within. Hence, I use the recurrent phrase or pointer *being within the space of the moment.*"

"Being within the space of the moment?"

"Yes. Though the first glimpse of this reality must be experienced, or realized, for it to be fully understood.

Remember nonetheless that the very opposite of what I here call spaciousness, namely mental contraction or suffering, often is not going on so much because of a physical circumstance as because of all the created mental-emotional turmoil, all that is being thought and felt around it. Suffering then occurs because of a non-accepting of what-is and of the craving for what-should-be."

"Being what you mean about 'self-created suffering'?"

"Exactly."

"But most of us can't help ourselves when being in a maelstrom state like this, can we?"

"It is strongly habitual and trance-like, yes, Simon, but self-inflicted nonetheless. Call it involuntary, mental contractions, or non-accepting movements uncontrolled stirring backward and forward between past and future, while that within you which always operates in the here and now is sadly overlooked. The very key to peace and freedom or to what Jesus repeatedly referred to his disciples as the 'Kingdom of Heaven within.'"

Zennis, from Bjørn Borg to Jesus. And a kingdom of heaven within. Game, set, and match . . . "And can an unforgiveable sinner like myself enter this 'Heaven'?"

Raman smiled. "Sin, or worthiness, has nothing to do about anything concerning Satsang and Awakening. Except maybe for the sin of steadily clinging to a state of ego-sleep and ignorance. So the answer is: Everybody can enter . . . at least in theory. But back to Zen, let's not forget that it is not at all about fancy words, rules, and theories; it is all about a living and breathing practice."

"Yes . . ."

"As with your half-completed Self-inquiry."

"Yes, but . . ."

" 'But' is always from the mind. Listen, when you say in your report that you see a 'me' wherever you inquire, it may be helpful to make a distinction in your set of concepts. Keep asking yourself, 'Who exactly is it that sees *me* as a bundle of thoughts and emotions?' And ask: 'To whom do these fragments of a shadow self, a *small me,* appear?' And whatever label you put to the revealing experience of a witness, you can also name <u>that</u> the *real me.*"

Small me and real me, discriminating, within the space of the moment. Suddenly I was enthused. Armed for internal battle. "Okay. Got you, Raman. Inquiry continues. Thank you. And about my Zen practice, besides meditation, where do I begin?"

Raman paused again. "Do you hear the waves breaking at the beach outside?"

"Clearly."

"Begin from there. Okay, Silvia?"

The new girl, Silvia, examined me. "Okay, Raman."

"*With no intention of pushing this fear away, or fixing it, analyzing it even, let's inquire closer into it. Let's not even name it fear. Let's say it is a vibration passing through the body.*"

Face Your Fear

Homework, my first task, or second if I included my ongoing inquiry, and I got it. *Waves of presence!* A momentary pride arose, and a brief childlike excitement, as if I were twenty-five years younger and a thirsty school-student again. Hours of wave-spotting, or wave-listening, more precisely, attentiveness to sounds in general, makes one stay out of the illusory past or future, holds one's attention to what-is, the here now! Sounds experienced not only as a reference point for presence, but also as potential pinholes in the mental lead curtain.

As the monsoon-rain kept pouring, the easy feeling didn't last. Lying on my madras bed in a humid rented room in a typical Indian backyard, listening to a crazy rooster, irritated not awakened, I was left with an aware-ness of again being full of mental activity, being un-centered. A relapse. Yet the new lingo was beginning to make sense. On my motorcycle rides in the breaks of rain I looked tentatively, not with *the small me*, but with *the real me,* at people passing. Spying up and down the streets, all of a sudden I had the revelation that everybody, including myself, was living life mostly in absence: somehow either in the midst of recalling the past or planning for the future. Physically here, but mentally somewhere else. No one was really present. Not at all awake to the momentary stream of life. It was a spooky revelation, like finding yourself as an involuntary actor in the latest film version of *Return of the Zombies*. Humanity lost in mind.

Staring at the fan in the ceiling. Not wanting to be where I was, and nowhere to go. Worries, concerns. Someone had turned the inside jukebox back on. Kind of creepy, because it wasn't me. Patti Smith's "Set Me Free" was running around in my brain: *Sometimes my spirit's empty; Don't have the will to go on. I wish someone would send me energy.*

Week's end. End of lingering. First on the spot and weighed down by gravity, I was waiting for the doors to the Kavalam residence to open. Without taking into account that maybe *I* occupied too much Satsang space, I was pondering about an elegant way to bring my excruciating state of mind up in tonight's meeting.

One by one, my fellow students arrived. The new girl, Silvia, on her bicycle, came right over, sat down with me, and scrounged a cigarette. I was only lukewarm, on guard, so to say. Another relational drama was not in my plans, but if she had an agenda she sure knew how to hide it. She tossed her hair and made a thin ring of smoke in the air. "I don't smoke, really."

"No. Smoking is not very spiritual, is it?"

She shrugged. "Nisargadatta smoked *bidis* all day long."

"Nisargadatta?"

"You don't know much, do you?"

"Nope, spiritually I am less than an amateur."

"Yet Raman likes you."

"What do you mean?"

"He sees your potential."

"Doesn't everybody have potential?"

Our eyes met. Brown, shades of green. She examined me while she quit smoking. "Not in this lifetime, they don't."

I hid a smile inside. "Ah, so you believe that maybe we have met before, somewhere in a previous life?"

She must have sensed my disbelief. Quite suddenly she got up and spoke, with another impressive toss of her hair. "Got to go, freshman. Somebody could give Raman the wrong impression . . ." She sent me an ambiguous smile. "And we wouldn't want that, would we? Anybody getting the idea that we are romanticizing in Satsang?"

Is that forbidden? She left me no time to ask. Leaving the scent of a woman in the air and some distressing words of recognition in my mind: *He sees your potential.* As the sitar was playing and I was waiting for Raman to enter the room, my mind was processing. I longed to drop the lead solder and again swim in the old captain's presence. And just before Raman's wheelchair parked, I came up with the following formulation: "Edvard Munch, the world-famous painter from my cold country, when finishing his masterpiece, initially wanted to name it 'Despair,' but the audience at the first exhibition spontaneously overthrew his decision. 'The Scream' it was, and as I speak I feel a scream of despair from somewhere deep inside. Sir, Doctor, Professor, Teacher, or Master, will you please once again accept me on your operation-table?"

The music stopped. My speech was ready. Raman opened his eyes, looked eagerly around: "Any questions?"

I waved, but so did a new face, a short-haired Australian woman. Raman ignored me and nodded at her, but she had not prepared like me. In fact, she had problems even uttering a whole sentence. "This . . . 'me,' Raman. I feel . . . feel . . ."

Raman looked encouragingly at her. "There seems to be a strong emotion attached to this question of yours. Let's look deeper into that emotion. Do you mind?"

To my disappointment Raman invited her toward him with his cane. And gently she sat down in the chair, was eventually able to speak. One word only. "Fear."

Raman smiled as if she was talking about a mutual friend. "Fear, yes. What is your name?"

"Karen."

"So, Karen, with no intention of pushing this fear away, or fixing it, analyzing it even, let's inquire closer into it. Let's not even name it fear. Let's say it is a vibration passing through the body."

"An unpleasant vibration, that is . . ."

"Can it be located?"

"Mostly in the stomach."

"Very good. In the stomach, something pulsating, shuddering. Imagine, Karen, let's say that it's liquid, almost, a pond with an agitated surface. Just allow it to be totally agitated. So . . . if you with your awareness dive into it, and sink . . . What do you find?"

She closed her eyes, struggled a bit, before she again was able to speak. "Pain."

"Good. Pain and sadness are deeper emotional layers than fear, but we have still not reached the only permanence, that which doesn't come and go . . . the firm ground that is beyond the surface of thoughts and the layers of emotion. What is at the deepest, Simon?"

I answered without thinking. "I am?"

"I am! So again, accepting the vibrations of pain as it is, not intending to change anything, allowing the awareness to drop even deeper, all the way down, like you were a pearl diver. What is there, Karen?"

She sat for a while with closed eyes, not moving. The whole room was waiting in excitement. Suddenly, out of nowhere, a little laughter.

"What is it?"

Karen smiled and laughed some more. "It's space . . . or joy, really!"

"Excellent. The *I am* as the *joy of being*. Which is never lost really, only covered, veiled, by thoughts and emotion."

Karen was baffled. "And all this—this veiling—because of fear?"

Raman nodded. "Fear fueling the lurking demons in the dark corners of your soul."

"I don't get it. What's the point of this fear?"

"In basic fight-or-flight situations, fear has its function. Pumping adrenalin for proper immediate action to be made. Beyond that, fear merely keeps humanity chained in a trance of emotional and mental absence."

"I would like to understand. How is that, exactly?"

"The memory of past pain sometimes appears as fear-thoughts, sometimes as fear-feelings. Or the sentiment that we are not going to get, or we are going to lose, what we think we need. Fear plus thought, plus more thought . . . and soon, outside the light of attention, a self-hypnotized drama overtakes the within. In fact, fear is the underlying emotion that governs most of the ego's activity. And in subtle ways it re-feeds itself by thoughts that hold the fear-emotion together. Does this somewhat resonate, Karen?"

"Yes."

"Yes. So, fully free of fear, ego-mind would lose its grip. A fearless mind is still, spacious, and clear, as a fearful mind is occupied, contracted, and noisy. So everybody, without thinking: What are you afraid of?"

"Snakes."

"Insanity."

"Nuclear holocaust."

"Women."

"Men."

Laughter. "Okay. All related, in the deepest core, to the fear of losing oneself, of losing control and being nobody, the fear of nonexistence, in its origin the primal fear of death, really. Problems occurring when this neuroelectrical defense impulse frequently acts in the brain and no death-related threat is present. The ego, then, in its programming handles this by a rush of mental activity, trying temporarily to cover up for these unpleasant vibrations. Often this dulling fear, fear of being or becoming nobody, then creates some kind of outer compensation: chasing another intimate relationship, for instance, or a new possession, overworking, being right or being best, alcohol, drugs, and screen-addiction."

I was hooked on Satsang. Even without asking, the answer was given. What I in all these years had been unaware of, now, in a flash, seemed crystal-clear. The very fuel to my ongoing agonizing internal hellfire seemed exposed: dulling fear. An unconscious fear that triggered streams of involuntary thoughts, an inner voice, and even repeating song lyrics, this rain-dance within creating obscuring clouds on my inner sky.

Raman looked at his audience with a glint in his eyes. "A man has been visiting a therapist for months, because he has a fear of monsters living under his bed. Every time he comes in, the therapist asks, 'Have you made any progress?' And every time, the man says, 'No.' The man decides to go and see another doctor. When he goes back to his first therapist and he again is asked, 'Have you made any progress?' he now answers, 'Yes, I am feeling all better now.' The therapist asks, puzzled, 'What happened?' The man says, 'I went to another doctor and he cured me in one session.' 'What did he tell you?' 'He just told me to cut the legs off of my bed.'"

Raman laughed. "Fear of an imagined future, of becoming less. Fear of rejection, of loneliness. Fear of the unknown, of freedom itself, even. Fear of fear. Man is the only being whose life is filled wavering with fear. It's like a spell. A divine hypnosis. And running away doesn't work: Escaping fear, avoiding it, it is attempted indefinitely, but it just haunts you. So how do you deal with fear, being on your own, when nobody is there to support you?"

"Admit it is there."

"Stay with it."

Silvia spoke: "When I have a mind-attack, I know it is always fear-triggered, and when putting the spot-light of awareness on fear—the passing feeling rather than the thoughts, and the passing vibrations rather than the feeling—it eventually, mostly, cracks like a troll in daylight."

"Good, very good."

Fear of fear, even? I raised my arm. "And what about fear and extreme mental states?"

Raman nodded. "The extreme frames of mind, mood swings out of the ordinary, highs and lows, may—and this is important not to overlook—cause or be caused by a chemical imbalance in the brain. But despite that, or in addition to that, they seem to be fear-based overoccupied mind-states more than anything. Psychosis may be seen as an explosion of mental activity, a fragmentation of mis-identities and thought patterns desperately trying to avoid or escape fear or angst. Depression is more of an implosion, a protective contraction, but quite often with the same escape-causality. Both states are causing people and their surroundings extreme suffering. In many of these cases, initially only treatment with medication may help. But a disease is not cured by dulling its symptoms, so after the chemical treatment it should be met like . . . How did you just do it, Karen?"

Karen giggled. "Cut the legs off my bed?"

Raman smiled. "More precisely?"

"Facing it?"

"Yes, you are chained to the fear only as long as you are trying to get away from it. Or are telling yourself a story about it. When met and accepted, without being charged as 'bad' or 'negative,' it changes into something else. The feeling simply does not perpetuate itself if it does not get any nourishment from the feeler behind it. So, fear faced: nothing but an unpleasant and passing vibration. And a possible gateway, even. Underneath the surface is, as we have seen, a freedom from clutters of thoughts and turmoil of emotion: space. Or joy of being. The very pearl you all have been looking for, isn't that so?"

"Yes."

"Okay then, Karen?"

"Okay, Raman."

"*Then the shift itself, suddenly, from a false mind-identity to full awareness of one's essence as pure consciousness. The veil of illusions, of maya, like a rolled curtain, lifted.*"

The Power of Presence

E *mancipate yourself from mental slavery. None but our-
selves can free our mind. "Redemption Song" buzz-
ing in my inner ear, even though Alappuzha didn't have
a Bob Marley bar and I had replaced hashish, alcohol,
and Ecstasy with another drug. I had become a junkie on
spiritual literature. A new world had opened, and I was
reading the Indian post-war big names: Ramana, Papaji,
Osho, and Ramesh. And Nisargadatta. Seemingly so different in all their splendor, yet still, each and every one
about the same. Consciousness. And the more I read and
pondered, the clearer Raman Kavalam's eminence became
to me. Not the least his capacity for keeping it simple,
for making the incomprehensible comprehensible. In
all modesty I was pretty well schooled in literature, psychology, religion, and philosophy. How come, then, any
of this about a higher consciousness wasn't commonly
known or accepted in the West? Was it simply because the
whole Western culture was sadly stuck in mind-fucking—
hung up in the old mental misconception of Descartes' "I
think, therefore I am"? For whatever reason, regarding the

human essence, the very core of our being, I concluded that Truth preferred an underground existence.

Rain-break and sunshine. I parked my motorbike in the shelter of an old banyan tree. Satsang time was here once again, and after another steep week I felt relief, but also guilt and some kind of numbness. The scream in my soul was toned down, as was the mental noise, but my ability to focus my attention was veiled, not only by my remaining mental stuff, but also by a small dose of chemical substance. Only 5 mg. in the morning, 10 mg. at night: I was on Valium.

Waiting for the doors to open, Silvia scrounged another cigarette. Dressed in Ali Baba trousers and a red top over a black bra, her skin color reminded me of maple syrup. Burned more than once, I really had no illusion of finding fulfillment in another relationship, even though the evenings were getting lonely. Compared to me, she obviously had a seniority in this spiritual area that attracted me. So on impulse, and in all innocence, I asked her for a coffee date. She looked at me, didn't answer, but smiled mischievously. I already regretted the initiative and felt exposed. *Could she read the Valium in my eyes, was that it?*

"What?"

She laughed. "Dulling fear of loneliness with an intimate relationship, maybe?"

Relieved on one level, I couldn't help being hurt on another. "Surely a married man like Raman doesn't preach celibacy or non-relating?"

She shook her head. "No, but picking up girls in Satsang isn't . . . *comme il faut.*"

"And why is that, exactly?"

"It comes across more like an escape than as a sincere process of dedicated inquiry, doesn't it?"

"I wasn't picking you up!" Hopelessly defensive, I could hear, I blamed my medication.

She gave me a sweet smile. "Coffee and then what, Simon?"

"How about two fellow seekers in mutual support, drinking coffee together, that's all. What's wrong with that?"

"Exchanging notes?"

"Exchanging friendliness!"

"Mmm. You're tempting me. I fill your void and you fill mine. I listen to your stories if you listen to mine?"

"No. Mutual . . ."

"Mutual story-confirmation. Need satisfying need. What's the presence in that?"

I felt uncomfortably undressed and apparently she had it even more than me. The force of disillusionment. "Wow, Silvia. Why relate at all?"

For a moment she held her tongue. Then she stood up. "*Why* is always from the mind."

Just like that, with Ali Baba hips, my unsuccessful dating-attempt walked out on me.

The sitar player had left for his family in the Himalayas. So no music, no introduction. Raman Kavalam gazed at me as if he could scan the chemical composition in my eyes, but then he looked just as strictly out over the other eleven people gathered in the Satsang room.

An Italian woman in her forties, whose name I didn't know, opened the verbal show. "Raman, I am frustrated. I am watching and watching thoughts, but they don't go away."

"Mind sometimes rebels against inquiry like that. This, too, will pass."

"But . . . it's kind of torturing, like an everlasting counting of sheep, or witnessing of clouds, but the sky never clears."

I tried to sharpen my attention, because this description, it could be me exactly.

"Okay, okay. So thoughts come and go, come and go. Don't charge them. Don't re-identify. Just let them pass. The 'sky,' or that which doesn't come and go, doesn't care about any obscuring clouds, does it? Or as the Native American saying goes: 'Rise above the clouds and the sun is always shining.'"

"So just stay witnessing, then?"

"Yes. Stay uninvolved. You can take it one step further, even. Ask yourself: Can this observing witness also be perceived?"

The Italian woman closed her eyes and paused. "I don't know . . ."

"So contemplate on that and be patient."

Perceive the witness? Beyond me. A middle-aged Indian man was next in line, waving his arm for attention.

"Yes, Sanjay?"

"Yes. I . . . I don't speak much, as you may have noticed, but I have been your devoted *sannyasin* for many years, Raman, and in this last period here I have been with you now every Friday for four months. And now I don't know how long . . . how much patience . . . Raman, swami, how come you have not yet made me awaken into a conscious living?"

In a momentary flash Raman changed expressions into something like a thunder-cloud. The unthinkable happened. Love and peace transformed itself into a tirade of fury.

"Basically, Sanjay, I am donating you a plow and an understanding of how to use it, but the plowing itself is up to you. It is all your responsibility! Waiving this in itself explains why nothing happens to you. Or to put it very clearly: What does it matter that I point out to you that the door to your prison cell is open, when your response is to hold on to your imprisonment and blame me for not carrying you on my back out of there? A student of inner Truth must never, ever make his quest any teacher's liability!"

Sanjay lowered his gaze and was as red as any Indian could get in his earlobes.

Raman's voice stayed in a harsher tone than usual. "So what is this that Sanjay expects me to hand him on a platter? Conscious living?"

Nobody dared to answer. Not Peter, not even Silvia. And for the first time I thought I could sense the physical pain in my teacher's eyes. I had heard that he had withdrawn from all medical treatment. Cancer was unstoppably eating his body up from within.

"Dinesh? Can you define consciousness?"

"Not in so many words, no . . ."

"Nobody?" I looked at the floor. Everybody did. *Stupid, really, this feeling of guilt, like an oppressive fog in my presence.* One of many conditioned reactions in my programming that I was becoming painfully aware of, bubbling to the surface.

Raman struck the cane furiously in the floorboards as an old-fashioned schoolteacher. "Silence? The silence of ignorance, that is, not to be confused with the silence of wisdom, which no words quite correctly can render full justice. So tell me the opposite, then, that which most of you experience in your everyday life: What is unconscious living?"

The assembly moved uneasily. Another thundercloud arose. As if we had committed a collective sin or something. Raman once more beat his cane on the table and swung his whip. "I see thinking eyes, eyes indulging in mind's realm, eyes in tune with only a small bit of consciousness: a fragment of who you are. Unconscious living is like that: helplessly identifying with thoughts and emotions, with the mental stream spinning back and forth between past and future, separating you from the space of the moment, from your true being. So in this moment you are either fully here or you are partly hypnotized by a bundle of 'me'-thoughts and thereby sadly being so much less than your potential!"

Raman looked forcefully out over his audience. "Words. Merely pointers. Nevertheless triggering some hint of recognition in you, perhaps?"

Provocatively so, and about potential, Raman's potential, I couldn't help thinking: *Such a shrunken body and yet so much power!*

A thundering speech, a stream of penetrating words, and no evidence of residence: "Truth is: Up 'till now you have been selling out for souvenirs, for a relative comfort sought in different, better, more, and the next thing, for nothing but transient substitutes of fulfillment. This unsatisfactory carousel will never change until you take a conscious responsibility for your own direction!"

Again the cane was hit on the table. This time it broke! There was a stunned hush among us all, and I couldn't help questioning, *Where is the consciousness in this kind of outburst of . . . anger?*

Raman looked at the broken cane and laughed, full-heartedly. We all looked at each other, but didn't quite dare to join in on the old captain's amusement. He looked undisturbed at each and every one of us; his voice was by magic again back to its usual softness. "Anybody with the courage to say something?"

I couldn't help feeling offended by his eruption and accusations, and I would argue that my mental programming, my software of conditioning, was outside my genes or hardware's control, but I didn't. Unsure as I was whether the metaphor measured up, unsure, and humbled. And that may very well have been the point of this unorthodox teaching, for what I knew. Ego-humbling.

Peter, eventually, was the brave one. He signaled and raised his voice. "Raman, how come all these powerful words happen through you if thoughts no longer appear in your mind?"

Raman smiled. "Good shot, Peter. A question that I will answer in all sincerity and to the best of my ability. Since the happening of my final Realization—and don't forget: I am an ordinary human being, and if it happened to me, it can happen to you—since my Realization, thoughts are often absent and definitely much fewer than before. Thinking, the horizontal stream between past and future, has completely lost its noisy grip, while vertical being, that which is in alignment with the present situation, has the undisturbed space. It could be said that an uncontrolled quantity of thoughts is replaced by a quality of present wisdom. That there is an unbroken presence, a peaceful awareness of 'I am' in the background of everything. So when thoughts do appear, there is no identification with them and they simply don't stick."

Raman grinned, and I was partly losing it again, my focus. For some reason I was thinking of my secret undisturbed place, of the tree by the river where I used to read, its bluish rattles with flowers which had become an attention for my meditation.

"Am I being rougher than usual on you tonight? Because you can't help your absent selves, can you?" Raman laughed teasingly. "*Leela*. The play of life. The source's own theater. A string of inputs and outputs. Or, as Shakespeare formulates it: 'All the world's a stage, and all the men and women merely actors playing their parts.'"

Shakespeare brought me back to presence. *What exactly was now being indicated? Another provocation: My life lived as a mechanical wire doll?* I had just about had it for tonight, with both Raman and his Satsang!

"Touché. And beloveds, kindred Selves, sometimes a good kick from a teacher is of more value to your growth and freedom than a thousand kisses. Don't forget that!"

I had read about that. An educational tradition going thousands of years back. The Zen master's stick-hit!

"And if perplexed, you now ask: 'What to do?' The answer being, on this stage, just hang on to the one who is *searching*. 'You are always the same unfathomable awareness, limitless and free, serene and unperturbed. Desire only your awareness,' from Ashtavakra Gita. A profound Hindu insight. The one who is *searching*? Who is that? At the end of the day you will find that the seeker is none other than consciousness seeking its source . . ."

I was about to lose my attention again. Valium dulled my fear-fuel, but obviously also my attendance. Raman made a dramatic pause before he continued. "What you are seeking is also seeking you. So the seeker himself is both seeking and the sought, and this comprehension may initially make both seeking and the seeker evaporate."

Searching, seeker, sought. The Who kicked in: *They call me The Seeker. I've been searching low and high. I won't get to get what I'm after 'till the day I die.* Another thirty-nine shadowy rotations around the sun? I missed out on a few Raman sentences and it was too late for a repeat.

Coming back to the now, I noticed Raman smiling a dry smile. "So, if this was an overload, let's clear up your confusion and establish a few definitions, or pointers, rather, about consciousness. Okay, Simon?"

I straightened my back. "That would be nice, Raman."

"Consciousness is always here, whether you are lost in your psyche or not. Without it, we wouldn't be sitting here and communicating. Acknowledged easiest, it is *the sense of being present, of being alive.* And yet it is so much more: Its many aspects are indicated by synonymous words such as awareness, spirit, Self, divinity, stillness, or even the force of godliness within. So far okay?"

"Yes."

Raman continued secretively. "So what then is the difference between the life force and consciousness which animates or possesses me and *that* which possesses you?"

I looked around, at a loss. Silvia concealed a grin and nobody looked back. It was awe in the room. Raman smiled teasingly and continued, "According to my understanding, no difference at all. In appearance, in physical and psychological makeup, yes, but in essence, there are no real separations between us, are there? Twelve beings, twenty-four eyes, but only one consciousness."

Could that be so? The same core in everybody? A concept triggering plenty of mental resistance I could feel. Confusion, even. For what, then, with my lifelong-held sense of being separate or different, unique? Despite my failures in life, I had always felt special somehow, and therefore also, as a life project, I had wanted to be someone out of the ordinary. To name a few adult roles: as a lover, as a college teacher, as a journalist, and not the least as a film director financing my own feature film. A feeling of specialness, notably to be confirmed sometime in the future, exactly from what I still owed private funders in Norway millions of crowns . . . *Nothing but "psychological makeup"?* I found that hard to accept.

Raman gazed around the room with a smile. "Now don't make another mental blocker of any of this. Just accept it as your old teacher's humble point of view that to fully realize the non-dualism and sacredness of life, you have to wake up from your dreaming of a better dream. You are still here, Simon, or dreaming?"

"Trying my best, Raman. To stay awake."

"Good. Because waking up is what my Satsang talks are all about. Firstly, preparing the ground in a gradual switch-over from thinking to awareness. Then, with the grace of the source, the shift itself, suddenly, from a false mind-identity to full awareness of one's essence as pure consciousness. The veil of illusions, of *maya*, like a rolled curtain, lifted."

Raman took a break, gathered his breath, and again looked slowly around his living room. We all sensed that he was touching the heart of his matter, the core of his life-dedication, and we sat like schoolchildren in breathless attention, awaiting some rite of passage to be transmuted to us.

"In the times of the Buddha, Lao Tzu, and Jesus, Awakening was apparently a rare happening. Today, not any more so. From all corners of the world, an increasing number of beings are now reported to realize their Selves.

A consciousness evolution. So have faith. More than anything what you need is a strong resolve to overcome your in-programmed self-harmful mental habits, your karma. So keep plowing, meaning keep learning to be more and more aware: aware of your actions, your thoughts, and your feelings. And when you are aware of all three, you will become aware of the fourth, which is awareness itself. This, since ancient times in India, is known as *sat-chit-ananda*. Translated from Sanskrit as being-consciousness-bliss. Or, more profoundly understood: beingness blissfully aware of itself as consciousness."

Foggy or not, again at the end of a Satsang, I felt uplifted. Of this uttermost human possibility existing, sat-chit-ananda, I was converted. Yet easier said than done, for sure. Even out of reach, almost certainly. *But halfway there would be worthwhile*, I was thinking. *Doubling equanimity, tripling aliveness?*

"And all these words, Peter, are unplanned. They really just happen, through the power of presence. Okay, Sanjay?"

"Okay, Raman."

"Perhaps a glimpse of pure presence already has happened to you. And of reduced living, spellbound in mental noise, you have had enough."

The Thirsty Few

Mental disruption. Perceptual reduction. Shades of gray. To whom does it appear, all this colorlessness? At least I wasn't suicidal anymore. But Shayamal, the chubby ten-year-old son of my landlords, sure had something I had lost. We were playing cricket between the puddles in the backyard. I tossed and he turned.

"You go to prayer tonight, Simon?"

"To Satsang? Yes."

Enthusiastic, he received a direct hit. "Yes! Why you go to prayer when you are not Hindu and free to play and do whatever you like?"

"I wouldn't call it prayer, exactly, or Hindu, for that matter."

"But you go every Friday to the holy man in the old villa down by the beach? Sri Raman Kavalam?"

I picked up the ball from under the porch. "Yes. I just like it, that's all."

Shayamal laughed. "Then you are his sannyasin."

"What does that mean, then?"

"That . . . he has gone all the way before you. And you follow. When he make you holy, you make me holy too, okay?"

"You would like that?" I tossed and he hit the ball over the rooftop, smiling broadly. "Yahoo! Everybody would like that." *In India, maybe. Holy? Shit.*

————◆◆◆————

Silvia avoided me. Neither did she stop by my seat outside the entrance for a cigarette. Nor did she return my long-distance smile or my greetings. It was all fine with me. Or so I deceived myself. *Seems like all relations sooner or later reach a point of frustration anyway. This one was just of the speedy sort.*

As the rain was pouring down outside the windows, the talk this Friday evening was dominated by a young Belgian woman. And there was hardly a male in the room not spontaneously falling in love with her, dressed in a sari as she was, and with quite a charismatic presence, a radiance of peace. With a French accent she said that a series of coincidences had brought her here, like pointing arrows. That she eventually had met an Austrian cavalier in Hampi "with an unusual look in his eyes" who had totally convinced her to change her route to come here, to Raman's Satsang. That this particular Friday just fitted with her returning back north to her flight to Belgium, but that she only had about thirty minutes available now before the night bus left for Mumbai. This was otherwise what she had to say: "Eventually, me being here, on an existential level, I know that everything that-is couldn't be any different. And it's like the Picasso quote: 'I don't search, I find.'"

"I don't search, I find!" Raman laughed a good belly laugh, and I noticed his cane being carefully glued together. "So if you couldn't have been any other place right now than right here, for sure you can relax and make the best of the situation. What is it that you want to know? Do you have any specific questions?"

She bowed. "On the bus ride down here, this consideration occurred in my consciousness of course, but it was not so easy to locate the question marks anymore. What eventually came up was that when I was a child I was taught to pray. So I guess this is still with me, and there is an unresolved question of the purpose . . ."

Raman frowned. "Look deeper. Let's say, for the sake of the special occasion, if you only had one question left to ask, what would it be?"

The young Belgian woman closed her eyes and looked within, slowly opening them again. She spoke in a low voice. "In that case, Mr. Kavalam, sir, I have all my life felt profoundly about the issue of Love and God, that in essence there is no diversity between the two of them?"

"Very good! What you are stating is that love is God and vice versa. Then what first has to be explored exactly is what you mean by the word 'love'. Does not 'love' imply a need of some kind? The 'love' between man and woman, for instance, satisfies the need of each for the other, doesn't it?"

Silvia turned her head and sent me a quick know-it-all look as Raman continued. "A need-love and merely the opposite of hate . . ."

The Belgian woman protested. "No, no. What I mean is a universal or impersonal love, that love that is refraining from any discrimination as 'mine' and the 'other.' "

"In other words unity, unity of being?"

"Unity is beautiful."

"Very good, and let it be added also that this is an ancient distinction. The split in Greek mythology between *eros*, lower or selfish love, and the love you are pointing at, *agape*, divine love, also so beautifully labeled as *caritas* in Latin."

I tasted the sound in my mouth. *Caritas*. Finally I had a word for it, for what I could so clearly sense contagiously pouring out of Raman's eyes.

"Then what exactly is this 'God' you are talking about?"

"God . . ."

"Wars have been fought over differences in understanding of this three-letter word."

"Yes. The very Source . . . of everything."

"Okay. The one without the other, as is the Hindu expression, but not to get stuck in differences of beliefs, and more interesting therefore; how exactly does this force manifest?"

She looked eagerly at him. "Yes! Knowing that exactly would be something! How, Raman?"

Raman was shining. "Is it not the very consciousness—the vital *aliveness* that we all constitute—because of which you are able to ask this question? Is it not the inherent force, with a variation of expressions, of *that*—this presence-love-god—one loves more than anything, because without it there is no existence? The consciousness in you and the consciousness in me: Are they not separate only as concepts, seeking unity, and is this unity-seeking not love?"

"Wow, Raman!" She was obviously moved.

"Now I understand better what St. John of the Cross, my longtime spiritual hero, meant by being anchored in the conscious presence that is Love, that is God, to 'dwelleth in God and God in him.'"

She smiled enthusiastically. Raman smiled likewise back at her. "*Sirr,* as the Sufis call it."

"Sirr?"

"According to Sufis, sirr is a secret substance within the heart of hearts, in the spiritual core of all beings, that is both the pilgrim and the path, and the essence of God's love for us all. This being why they often great each other with this, their highest principle: '*Ishq Allah Ma'bud Allah.*'

'God is Love, Lover, and Beloved.' Or, a little simplified, if you like: 'Love loving love.'"

Raman's answer brought tears to the young woman's eyes. "Love loving love is God. How beautiful! What then is prayer, and what is the purpose thereof?"

"Illness is not cured by reciting the word 'medicine,' as Enlightenment is not achieved by repeating the word 'God.' Except as a meditation-practice, prayer, as it is generally understood, is nothing but begging for something."

The young Belgian woman spontaneously gathered her hand-palms in a traditional Namaste greeting. "Thank you. I feel like, like some concluding nonsense has dropped off."

"Do you mean that you seem to see everything clearly?"

"Not 'seem,' sir. It is clear. I am . . . *that*."

"*Who* is *that*?"

She laughed. "*Who* cares?!"

Raman smiled like I have hardly ever seen him smile before. "Excellent. Meaning there is no longer an ego-identity there to be concerned." She shook her head and Raman proceeded. "So know this: Tests will occur as the old identification attempts to reestablish. Don't take the bait, as both inner demons and the outer herd, in so many ways, will try to lure you back to mental slavery. Stay vigilant and ignore it. May thoughts and emotions from now on appear and disappear within you like nothing more than how sound waves play out and display within the graceful space of silence."

"Merci, Raman."

"Very good. A further soul broken free is for the benefit of us all." Raman closed his eyes for maybe a minute. We all closed our eyes. Part of me was in excited support, as another part of me couldn't help feeling the unpleasant feeling of envy. I glanced furtively at her as she sat with her eyelids lowered, and I really could sense it, some kind of an invisible glow.

For a short while longer she remained unmoving, obviously touched by the moment. Then she stood silently up and gathered her sari. She bowed to Raman and, in my reminiscence, floated out of the room. Raman Kavalam looked delighted after her. He waited maybe another minute in silence before he again addressed the remaining congregation. "For many years, my life was a rollercoaster in mental states, and somehow I was a seeker without even being aware of for what. Eventually, when my spirit again was low, it was love, in the shape of my wife, who brought me to my first Satsang. A direction was gained, yet there was a long karmic journey still to go."

Raman laughed. "Becoming and being a seeker is a mystery. It may involve experiences alternating from peaks of joy to valleys of hell, but there is no choice to it, really. If you try to escape, and you probably have, sooner or later it will whisper in your heart yet again. Or it will grab you by the throat. Love searching love, consciousness attracting consciousness, and Self seeking Self. It's a longing toward your unknown fulfillment. Often I get questions about good and bad teachers, but from my point of view it is more a question about good and bad students, really. In a well-known comparison, students have been categorized as either gunpowder, charcoal, or wet wood. There are some aspiring psyches which are like gunpowder, which need but one spark of the fire of wisdom from the lips of the teacher to set them free. While there are others so wet that they are not capable of responding even to a blazing fire. What about you, Peter?"

Peter grinned. "Thanks a lot, Raman. As you know, it took quite a while. Still, I say I was more in the middle, like charcoal."

"And you, Prawesha?" Raman addressed an elderly Indian woman with long gray hair who was always smilingly present in Satsang. Receiving this question, her smile turned into laughter. "Almost twenty years of seeking before meeting you, Raman, and now four years with you, I would say wet wood, soaking wet!" Everybody laughed. And I couldn't believe it. There were at least two more enlightened souls in the room, confirmed, and I knew one of them! *If it could happen to them . . .*

Silvia met my eyes for the second time this Satsang, but this time I couldn't read her expression. She turned and waved her hand to get Raman's attention.

"Yes, Silvia?"

"What then is spiritual ripeness or spiritual maturity?"

"Yes . . . imprecise terms, really. Some people wake up out of nowhere, without doing the slightest bit of practice for such an 'achievement.' Even though for most of us it is a process, a growth, which in the most fortunate cases sooner or later means reaching what could be called the point of no return. When the tendency to relapse back into experiencing your Self merely as thoughts and emotions loses its grip . . . But I have the feeling you already know this, Silvia, so why do you ask?"

Silvia met Raman's eyes without answering, without saying a word. The moment was getting awkward, but not for Raman, apparently, who eventually nodded confirming to her. "Do you have a word for your response?"

"Stillness."

"Stillness, yes. Or consciousness without thought."

Silvia failed to hide a smile. "Sir, does this mean . . . ?"

"Wait and see, Silvia. Or rather, let it be, and then see."

"But . . ."

"Let it be, and let go."

Silvia seemed to want to protest, but he ignored her.

I was pondering seriously whether I was to end in the category of charcoal or wet wood as Raman had one more point to make to the rest of us. "Gunpowder, charcoal, and wet wood . . . differences that still don't separate what I call a good student from a bad one. A variation in karmic baggage only. Because in this room, you all have something else in common, don't you? The most necessary quality? Like Peter and Prawesha and this young woman with whom we so beautifully just shared our consciousness?"

He smiled teasingly. "If you don't know, really know, deep down, *what you want*, you just float around on the surface of life, don't you? Controlled by subconscious desires, by genetic impulses, and society's conditionings. So that's why I say for the rest of you: Perhaps a glimpse of pure presence already has happened to you. And of reduced living, spellbound in mental noise, you have had enough. That a force of disillusionment with the prison of normality is operating gracefully in your life. In summary, you hold the only requirement necessary: a thirst for truth and a yearning to be free. The upward aspiration."

Raman paused and looked at us. He took a deep breath. "It is my firm observation, as a spiritual teacher of nearly three decades now, that a Realization of the Self, in theory, is available for everybody, yet in practice reserved for *the thirsty few* . . ."

"Okay, Prawesha?"

"Okay, Raman."

"Initially what needs to happen is a let-go,
a tensionless, silent state of being."

Limitations of Mind

I'll probably never understand why Cat Stevens changed his name and stopped creating his beautiful music, but I suddenly understood why he sang: *Oh I can't keep it in, I can't keep it in, I've gotta let it out.* Chilling outside on my porch after the rainstorm, suddenly existence switched to full color. A few raindrops were making magical circles in the luminous puddle. An outer radiance somehow originated by an intense wellbeing and fragile quietude within, a *sound of silence.* I gazed cautiously, as in slow motion, all around in the backyard as if some kind of energy, or a secret light, was shining from within everything. I had no idea how long this, this supernaturalism, lasted. I didn't dare to look at my wristwatch.

As it all had faded, I was left back in the shadows with my life's most intense remembrance and a handful of intrusive questions. *What happened? What did I do? How do I make this intense peace re-arise? Arise more long-lasting or even permanently, if possible?* Excited I was having a cappuccino with Peter before Satsang.

"Sounds like you had a taste of it, of presence's nectar, yes, a so-called *Satori* moment." He laughed. "So much stronger, yet a little like sex and orgasm, isn't it? In the sense that 'till you have had your first direct experience, everything is just hearsay and theory. You now *know* what Raman is pointing at."

"I do? Okay . . . and now what do I do?"

"Yes, that's the question, isn't it? I can tell you what not to do. When you have had a glimpse like this and you search for another—a repetition—it is automatically being objectified in your mind. Consciousness is not an object in mind to be grasped or found, and also it is already in the past. Mental dust. So my advice is to let the memory go, sweet as it is, and as always, return your meditative attention back to the present opening into this indefinable formlessness."

It made sense, I guess, but was kind of disappointing, actually. Back to square one. Except for one major difference. All further talks of awakening my Satori now made for a convincing clarity. *It* exists and *it* is possible. And having the wisdom of lasting Awakening at my café table, I couldn't help myself for asking. "If you are already Realized, Peter, why are you here? Still in school, so to say? And Pravesha? And Anand, maybe?"

"For some of us, certain *vasanas*, unresolved tendencies, are still an issue, and more generally we are all drinking of Raman's well. An urge for a never-ending deepening is still with me, and also a life-lasting gratitude toward Raman. Even though my path is that of *jnani* more than anything—the path of Realization through knowledge and insight—I fully understand the Indian seekers, who I believe are more into the path of *bhakti,* of devotion, to the teacher and to divinity as such. And they of course also have this special thing about hearing their teacher's last words . . ."

Silvia approached me only five minutes before the Satsang doors opened. Apparently we were on speaking terms again. Dressed in tight-fitting green, she again scrounged a cigarette.

"Are we friends again, Silvia?"

"We were never not friends, Norwegian darling. It's not because I do not like you that I have kept away. Or because of any unwritten Satsang rules, for that matter."

"No?"

"No. Heard about your Satori, by the way."

"Yes, it was something else, I tell you. Convincing stuff. Mind-blowing, like . . ."

She laughed. "I have had a few bliss-outs myself. The first ones are usually most spicy. Probably because they have the strongest contrast between being seriously mind-fucked, 'being normal,' as it is culturally celebrated, and suddenly being encountered with a free fall into an inner empty sky. A nirvanic bungee jump in spaciousness, so to speak. Welcome to the ranks of the half-baked!"

She somehow threw me off center, as when I was twelve and was blushingly talking to the fourteen-year-old girl next door who, according to rumor, had done it. Silvia looked at me and laughed at my expression. "Pity there is no technique to just repeat it, isn't it, Simon?"

"So I hear. Peter merely points to the opening in the present, the space of the moment."

She leaned against me. "Do you know tantra?"

Only the inner circle of chairs was occupied in the Satsang room. Nine people only. I couldn't believe it. As far as I was concerned, history was written, spiritual history, at least. Records of truth. I was still a bit high on my taste of presence's nectar. Raman opened the shrinking congregation as always, by meeting everybody's eyes. The bad showing didn't seem to bother him a bit.

"Let's all get warmed up by a small story about Aristotle and Heraclitus, and then we will see where tonight is going. Aristotle, one of the greatest thinkers of all time, is in the routine of walking up and down his private beach with a long, serious face, being really close to once again solving the problems of the universe, when all of a sudden he is being disturbed. A half-naked bearded man is doing something in the left corner of his beach. Reluctantly Aristotle steps out of his own footsteps, approaches the trespasser, and discovers that the man has made a hole in the sand the size of a football and is now carrying water in a cup up from the ocean and pouring it determinedly into the hole. Aristotle clears his throat. 'My dear man, you are trespassing, what exactly do you think you are doing?' Heraclitus pours in the water and goes steadily down to the waves to get some more: 'I was planning to fill all of the ocean into this hole,' he explains. Aristotle laughs, which didn't happen very often. He points to the hole: 'And how exactly are you going to fill all of the ocean, all its vastness, into this?' Heraclitus stops, smiles, and taps Aristotle on the head: 'And how are you going to fill the whole universe into that?'" Raman smiled. "Point being? Silvia?"

"Something about the limitations of mind."

"Limitations, indeed. The perceptual and cognitive functions of our brain can for instance not grasp infinity, the nothingness before the Big Bang, or that no matter is really solid, but merely whirls of energy. Nor can it grasp, as shown in the world of quantum physics, that the universe is made up of an interconnected unbroken wholeness where all particles, as energy waves, interact and there is no such thing as empty space; all is full of 'zero point energy.' Nobody, not even Aristotle, knows the cosmic law, the will of the source, or, as Einstein put it: the mind of god. So, then, can anybody's mind fully comprehend consciousness? Silvia?"

Silvia smiled. "No, not possible. Mind appears within consciousness. Consciousness therefore can observe mind, but not the other way around. Our comprehension of consciousness, if there is any, must be from consciousness itself."

"Very good, nor can mind observe itself. A thought cannot, as it occurs, self-reflect. Summarized, one can say that consciousness exists fine without mind, but mind cannot exist without consciousness. Mind, ego, the 'me'—more precisely a bundle of thoughts and emotions—is indeed a limited identification."

Raman made a reflection break before he continued. "What else does the story possibly tell us? Something about mind's attachment, isn't it? In this case, the inordinate need to have something occur in a specific way, at a specific time, in a specific sequence. When we, unlike going with the flow of life, notoriously expect things to come about in a certain way, we become attached to that predetermined next step, and through this often we are completely blind to new ways that something can come about. Even if an enlightened genius like Heraclitus appears in our presence, we might very well miss the opportunity, wouldn't we? Meeting life with closed doors. Missing out on a possible Awakening happening, even."

Raman looked at me. "Let's play a little game. Simon, will you come up here?"

Yes! I was thrilled to be sitting with him again, to feel like his pet, and to be swimming in his eyes on close rank. My newfound experience was burning inside, but somehow he already seemed to know. "Let's say yours has been a long and arduous journey, Simon. Now, almost reaching the end, there is a test: a broad and streaming river to cross. From where you are standing, if you can't reach the other shore, you will have to return all the way back on your journey the same way you came. And if, or when, you are pushing the river, so to speak, and trying to go against the current, against the suchness of existence, you will feel an increasing mental and physical tension. Maybe angst even wearing you down. The only good news being: A tiny boat awaits you, but as it is, it cannot carry you over. You are too loaded. What will you do?"

"Drop the baggage."

Raman looked surprised at me. "What baggage, exactly?"

"The dust of my past and the projections of the future."

Raman drummed the glued cane with recognition in the floor. "A very Zen answer, indeed, but the question remains: Who would do that?"

"Me . . ."

"Can a nonappearance of 'me' be done by the same 'me'? Can thoughts undo themselves? When this kind of doing is tried, is it not with an apparent, or hidden, sense of personal doership or sublime pride even? Remember: One mental gram is enough! Enough ego-weight to make you sink halfway over. A nice try, Simon, but there is a more dependable way out of this final dilemma. Another answer to the riddle. I'll give you a hint. The boat for your last crossing's name is 'Sweet Surrender.'"

If the hair on my neck could rise, now was it. *Sweet Surrender?*

Raman giggled. "The boat cannot carry the heaviness of a personal identification, more precisely especially that part of the ego we could call the false sense of control. For even though great teachers of spirituality throughout the centuries have used the words that mind has to be destroyed, in my understanding the mind-computer doesn't in any way have to be deteriorated, only the identification with it as *who you are* needs to be broken. Mind as such can be a beautiful instrument for its use, also after a permanent Awakening, but as a servant, not the master. So what would you do, Simon?"

Again Raman's words hit me exactly where I was at. This time, explaining probably why my little Awakening happening couldn't last: because of an unbroken attachment to my personal identification. A *me* ready to jump in and make any experience *mine*. Clarity, yes, but at the same time it felt far outside my power to influence any of this. Forces just made it happen this way. "In my case, Raman, if the alternative was going back the same way I came, back to depression, back to a suicidal mental suffering,

I would probably, even without knowing the consequences, surrender."

Raman smiled. "Probably?"

"Yes, honestly, it feels too hard to give up without knowing the consequence."

"Okay. Okay. I know Westerners generally have more of a problem with the word 'surrender' than Easterners. As if Churchill should have surrendered during the Nazi *blitzkrieg*, right? Spiritual surrender is first and foremost an indispensable step in silencing the ego-mind and in no way the same as quitting or giving up. You give up to a struggle and surrender to an inner embrace. And also, in the very same operation, meeting life, as an unconditional acceptance of this moment, without pushing or wrestling and struggling with it. Laying down your arms against the suchness of manifestation, so to speak. A psychic relaxation at its deepest, really."

I could still feel my own resistance. "And if I don't like it? What's happening in this moment?"

Captain Ram halted and met nine pairs of eyes. Nodding, it became obvious that he was gaining time, that he had another pain-attack, a torture going on somewhere in his internal organs. Finally he gained his strength. "You still accept that it is here, Simon, and simply respond. True surrender is the inner transition from resistance to acceptance for whatever comes your way, the hardships as well as the joys."

Almost physically I could feel his pain as he spoke, and who could argue with that then?

"Spiritual surrendering, Simon, apropos of the limitations of mind, is no more mystical than a letting-go to some deeper sense of existingness than your own personal agenda. It might take some courage to begin with. In your case you could even consider it as a challenge."

"Okay."

Raman smiled. "Okay? So how would you 'probably' surrender?"

"To you?"

He shakes his head, smilingly. "A common misunderstanding, that a subordination to another being is needed. You are welcome to use me as a symbolic device, or more precisely the divinity that possesses me, but my suggestion for you to ultimately conquer yourself, Simon, is to find your own symbolic way to surrender your head to your heart—your spiritual heart, that is—submitting your mentality to your divinity within."

Why is this so hard? As if I have anything to lose, really? Anything but my depressing self-image? A challenge . . .

Raman focused his eyes on me. "Why '*Sweet* Surrender,' by the way?"

"I don't know."

"'Don't know' is good; it is an open mind-state. 'Sweet Surrender,' because what starts to happen within as you surrender your fictional control is that you put the burden of your struggling down. Tensional resistance gradually evaporates and suffering starts to drop off. Peace and joy, maybe even bliss, are the final consequences of surrender, and misery the consequence of an ongoing resistance, a clinging to your closed mental image. So what is going on right now, Simon? Give me some feedback."

I hesitated, but I didn't want to burden either Raman or tonight's Satsang with more of my mental disturbance, my recurring doubt.

"Have faith, sir?"

"Faith? In freedom?"

"Yes."

"Okay, that's the only sort of faith that will do. Put all your existential capital on that one horse, then, and make the Self fall in love with you. I see you, Simon. Your essence shines through. Sweet surrender is awaiting you by the riverside."

"Thank you, Raman."

"Okay, Simon. Good enough. You may find your seat."

As I sat down, and as Raman continued, my eyes met Silvia's, and if I didn't know better I would have read her expression as jealousy. Raman summarized: "Take away all your strategizing, judging, labeling, liking, disliking, explaining, or rehearsing, and your mind is clear as space. What I enjoy calling the human biogenetic computer is run by many programs to whom a direct switch-off button for thousands of years has been sought, yet not found. Hardwired as it is with a habitual fear to lose control. Nevertheless . . . in any quest for spiritual growth, initially what needs to happen is a *let-go*, a tensionless, silent state of being."

A let-go? So that's what by itself just happened in the backyard? Raman looked suddenly exhausted.

"Enough for tonight . . . Okay, Anand?"

"Okay, Raman."

"If there is any formula at all to discovering the Truth of who you are, it lies in the distinction between an occupied mind and a still, or clear, mind."

Enlightenment How?

*T*he gate is straight. *Deep and wide. Break on through to the other side.* According to the Doors. And . . . if a woman asks you whether you know tantra, make sure you know what you are going along with. In the case of Silvia Sender, I was invited in on a supposedly "unifying cosmic experience." Meaning the two of us sitting naked on the rooftop, me in lotus position, her motionless on my lap. And with my *lingam* blissfully united with her *yoni.* Yet that was not at all that it was about. Merging and synchronized breathing, so I learned, was a possible gateway to divinity; inhalation imagined through my heart chakra and out through our connection point. Her breathing, rhythmically circle-responding, in through her root chakra and out through her heart. Breaking on through, like starring in a film, *Being Jim Morrison.*

Unified under the stars in an energy-firing circle. Lingam to yoni, breath to breath and eye to eye. But gazing into Silvia's eyes was not like looking into Raman's spaciousness. There was definitively someone there wanting something. Through the eye-gazing, she whispered: "Can you feel your presence, Simon?"

I choked on laughter and whispering back, I couldn't help myself. "Something . . . enclosed and wet?"

"Don't be silly, be still!"

Expecting nirvana at any moment? Unified as we were, lower and higher, and me gazing deep into the mirror of her determined soul, what could possibly be wrong? Well. No kissing, no touching, and sitting motionless like this and circle-breathing, maybe for half an hour already, I was slowly obtained by biological laws. I had a choice between keeping the meditation and slowly shrink into an unplugged end or to create some friction. Tentatively I tightened my lingam. Silvia sat just as unmoving and goddess-like with her hot yoni all around me. *The spirit is willing, but the flesh is weak.* Larger forces took charge. Starry sky or not, it was one-way traffic and I knew it.

Getting dressed, she started teasing me. "You're not much of a tantra man, are you, Simon?"

"If that means to completely give up simply enjoying the gift of sex, no thanks." As I put my trousers on, everything about her began to irritate me—that I still found her so attractive, especially. Secretly, I admired her Cleopatra-neck as she tied her hair up in some kind of queen-like arrangement, and I could have bit my tongue as I heard myself saying, "We could try again?"

"Tantra, darling, is for those on the verge of higher consciousness, for those who no longer are being slaves of their animalistic drives."

I snapped back, "And your problem, darling, spiritually not least, is trying too hard!"

Silvia looked at me with, I could swear, a teardrop in the left corner of the right eye. She departed my roof without a word. Leaving behind only . . . somewhere I had read that the female excretes an odor for the male's entrapment. A silly thought. I closed my eyes and tried to meditate.

An hour later I opened my eyelids again. A shooting star caught my eye in the southern sky and, as was my habit, I again took stock. I had quit the Valium with neither angst nor depression reappearing. I was doing Zazen one to two hours a day. I was reading my spiritual books and walking presently on the beach and in the forest. And, not least, I had had my first taste of presence's nectar. No void was begging to be filled. Neither fear of loneliness nor any mental, emotional, or physical need of company was running my show. Even the smell of young Miss Sender had evaporated. Stillness was near and I was thirsty for a freedom that, only a few weeks back, I didn't know existed.

What worried me was Raman's condition. Week by week, his body was literally shrinking. Only his audience was expanding. All of a sudden it was nearly thirty participants in the Satsang room, apparently in attendance to pay their last respects. Or, according to Peter, before he departed, they came to see a dying Master.

Raman opened the evening with a quote: "'Cannot grasp it, cannot rush it. It is unattainable, and yet you too can attain it.' Written by the Zen master Aka Genkaku, some thirteen hundred years ago. Words of experienced insight, of Realization, eternally true. So if Genkaku's koan-like expression is right, and on this there is no reason to give space for the as always doubting mind, then the key question remains: What to do when it is unattainable? Why not stay in bed and pray on the pillow for the grace of the source? Mariana?"

Mariana was a Dutch lady in her late thirties and old student of the captain who had just arrived in Alappuzha. She gave her teacher a warm smile. "So grateful to again be in your Satsang-presence, Raman. Staying in bed, or any other kind of laziness, gives space for boredom, and thereby an unfortunate thinking activity in the mind. Negative spirals often. Better, then, whether on the spiritual path or not, to do something that stimulates presence and helps emptying the mind of polluting thoughts."

"Exactly. Your mind is either quiet or noisy, and if there is any formula at all to discovering the essential Truth of who you are, it lies in the distinction between an occupied mind and a still, or clear, mind. Spiritually, it doesn't really matter what kind of internal dialogue the mind is occupied with, only that its occupation and chattering means that it is blocked for deeper insight. And any deep understanding, any transformation, can happen only in a still mind. For the sake of clarification, you may say that what I call Awakening, Self-realization, or Enlightenment, presupposes a vacant space within for *it* to appear in." Raman paused. "So if Realization directly is unattainable and cannot be done because the ego cannot undo itself and any such effort means a tension or a strategizing that itself is an aspect of the same unwelcomed, identity-dominating ego. That it is like a snake biting its own tail or a catch-22. So, then, what to 'do'? Like Mariana says, something that stimulates presence! The simple litmus test being if you are getting more silent, more peaceful, more calm, more loving or joyful, you are on the right path. And vice versa? Not."

Taking a good look within, I felt calmed. With a few minor setbacks, pop-up images of maple-syrup skin, mostly, I was on the right track. Raman continued. "So to all you newcomers—some probably attending Satsang for the first time, even—you are all welcome to warm your bones by my fire. In recent weeks I have spoken thoroughly about such spiritual essentials as *mind and consciousness, facing fear, Self-inquiry, surrender,* and *Zen.* And since grace does not cherish the lazy, tonight's pointers are an old sage's handful of additional guidelines. A toolbox to still your mind. Procedures for Realization. Particularly for *you* to happen."

Raman spent a few minutes looking resolutely at everybody. As his old eyes met mine, I could feel in a flash and beyond doubt that he really meant it. For everybody in the room to reach a lasting Awakening. "Truly, I don't plan my talks too much, but on these topics I admit I had intended to use more than one Friday night, being as it is though . . ." Raman gave us a fatalistic smile and we all knew what he was implying.

"We love you, Raman!"

Raman took a long breathing-break before he continued. "Most Awakenings, with no comparisons, take place under the guidance of an *enlightened teacher*. The ancient metaphor is that of the teacher as a lit oil-lamp and the student as an unlit. And when 'the wind is favorable,' the flame transmits. *It* in a sense is contagious and in *Tirukkural*, the masterpiece of Tamil literature, it is written: 'Attach yourself to Him who is free from all attachments. Bind yourself to that bond in order that all other bonds may be broken.'"

Raman paused. "The question then has been pondering in seekers' minds for thousands of years: 'Who is the right teacher for me?' Eventually only you can know the answer, but it is my position that a good student can wake up with a mediocre teacher, but a mediocre student cannot wake up with a good teacher. With this said, a right teacher is someone Awakened, of course—someone with a strong presence and a clarity in understanding—and with no unresolved tendencies regarding power, sex, or money. Trust and resonance is of uttermost importance. For some, love is a key. And too much seriousness is a sickness!"

Everybody laughed. "What is the teacher's basic function, Raman?"

"The prime function of a spiritual teacher is not all unlike the sculptor who is hacking away that portion which prevents the final vision from being seen. Or you can say that the teacher assists the seeker in removing that which separates her from the Truth of who she already is. That he shows her that she is not what she thinks herself to be. In different ways he reflects who he is, *that*, to her experience of what she is and points her to her true essence. A recognition of the Self."

Not an eyelid moved as these words sank in. Raman was already breathing heavily. "Next: *Meditation*. There are some hundred techniques. Different ways to observe your mind silently without any judgment. Pick one according to your likings. And once you get a knack of it, your whole life can be filled with the same watchfulness. Observing thoughts passing by; such a pleasant sharpening of awareness. But a spiritual practice should be done by heart, not as a mental push. And meditation is an instrument to still the mind for a let-go to happen, not a means unto itself. It is a bridge to get you across the last canyon. A seeker once proudly told me that he had been doing the same refined meditation daily for ten years. Sadly, what he had done was being addicted to his practice and building a house on the bridge."

As always, Raman had his thirty students' utmost attention, but his breath made dangerous and scratching sounds in his lungs. "*Relaxation.* As so poetically has been spoken: Relaxation is the very soil in which the roses of Enlightenment grow. Because the ultimate state prior to the state beyond states is a melting point, an absence of the 'me' fearing or wanting nothing, isn't it? So in fact a seeker can be said to be living in the future, searching for a future Realization to happen. Yet she must never forget that the final Realization can only happen in the space of the moment. At a certain point, then, for instance *now*, all searching has to be dropped. All wanting, even the aim of Enlightenment, is a load too much, a tension or a mental contraction, and thereby a conclusive hindrance."

I looked at Silvia, but Silvia didn't look at me. This was her what-she-needed-to-hear, I was sure! But did she get this, or was she in some kind of denial, I wondered?

"Relaxation doesn't necessarily mean doing nothing. Boredom, as already highlighted, fertilizes the mind. Doing something extraordinary to relax is also often not the best way. Joyfully experiencing daily activities is fine, without a sense of doing, tuning in with the source."

Satsang was different with so many attendants, I was thinking. Less intimate, more of a lecture. Raman looked pale. "*Aloneness.* I have no attitude about sex or relationships. If it happens, it happens, and if it doesn't, it doesn't. Yet I must rush to add that I have never heard about anyone waking up as they were chatting with friends in a café, on their cell phones, or on the Net, or as a result of holding their lover's hand for that sake. You are born alone, you will die alone, and in between, relating or not, you are with yourself, alone. The word 'alone,' in fact, comes from 'all one' and has in it the potential of being 'one with all.' And aloneness: enjoying your own company, and loneliness: not standing being just with 'me,' are not to be confused. They are quite different matters. Periods of true aloneness are crucial in any authentic seeker's life. Being unplugged and spending time alone may for some of you be frightening. But if you, like far too many, are dulling your fear of loneliness by constantly being entangled in the other, playing the me-and-my-important-relationships-tape on internal loop, spiritually your life will be wasted, as your Self will stay forever buried and forgotten!"

If anybody was dozing, the last words sure made them wake up. Raman gave us a teasing smile, in pain. "Briefly summarized, what you in the core of your heart are looking for . . . the deeper secret of life, tends to open its door only in solitude."

By these provocations he looked over and done with, but yet he was obviously not finished. I felt an urge to come to the rescue. For the first time in Satsang, I simply knew where the teacher was heading. "What about nature?"

Raman nodded, got a spark of new energy. "Not to forget. There is no teacher greater than *nature*. We need the natural to show us the way home, the way out of the cage of our artificial minds. Birds singing, trees wavering in the wind, and water in motion. Allow nature to shower your soul and point you back home: to your stillness within, veiled as it is, but never lost."

The Satsang room was so silent, I could hear not only the waves, but also the birds singing outside. By the grace of the source, Raman's flat batteries gathered another spark and another handful of punch lines rolled out of the mystery-bag. "In a traditional analogy of walking the path, it is said that our ego-attachment is like a pair of shoes. Without such shoes, we wouldn't start out on the path, although as we walk along, we find that our shoes begin to bother us, break down, and wear away. But if someone told you to toss out your shoes right at the beginning, you most probably wouldn't listen, you would be offended. Even so . . . less usual than the gradual path, there is an immediate path available this very moment. Right here!"

Raman kept us on the rack. "Existence is here, you are here, yes, even more so, even if all mental activity is detached. All you have to do is to stop feeding your last thought and shift your attention to the silence in which any thought appears. Stop to that which already is at peace within. Rest in awareness and be still. Let's say for one tiny minute, only. Starting right now!"

There was an uneasy movement in the crowd, but Raman was sincere, and as silence filled the crowded room, I could already witness the first thought coming. And with that a thought about a thought. Filters, like patterns of rain on the window. Not to be given any attention, to be seen right through . . . the experience of, on the teacher's command, not being able to be internally still even for one minute was humiliating. I sneaked a look and met Silvia's open eyes and I could swear I sensed a glimpse of frustration and maybe even fear as Raman, sixty torturing seconds later, completed tonight's session: " 'This mad mind does not stop. If it can stop, that itself is Enlightenment, that itself is nirvana.' So spoke the Buddha already some twenty-six hundred years ago, and in this sense nothing has ever changed. So as you keep purifying your house, don't forget the comprehension that you are not your mental interiority, not a bundle of cravings and aversions. This profound insight need not be a matter of further yearlong and gradual practice. Why should it take any time at all, really, to fully absorb that you are so much richer than the pity voice in your head? Okay, Mariana?"

"Okay, Raman, beloved."

"All experience is simply passing through us in the same way that the Earth, Water, Fire, Air, and Space elements are flowing through our physical form."

Contemplation of the Six Elements

I hadn't met Silvia the passing week and now she was nowhere to be seen. Also, the bicycle was gone. She was not in Satsang, and I could feel her unexpected absence as an unforeseen sting. With this, and with Peter gone, and with the room full of newly arrived strangers, it was as if low pressure were building up on my inner sky. The last days' additional demon, variations of a reappearing doubt, came lurking now also into my usually so peaceful waiting-for-the-teacher meditation. Wasn't all of this, this more or less desperate project, Enlightenment nonetheless, maybe way out of reach for a petty criminal from Oslo?

Raman greeted another old student, Jennifer from Auckland, New Zealand, several people were waving their arms, and it was noisy in the temple. A big man, a first-time stranger, made his way rather forcefully from the back of the packed Satsang room. "Raman! Raman, sir, I am sorry to burst in like this. I just arrived today all the way from the States and I have an urgent question I just have to ask." He was bearded and in his fifties and Raman, undisturbed, allowed him to coup the attention. "The case is I have been going from teacher to teacher now for many years and I have had many experiences of awakening, but they just don't last. Every time I go back to my ordinary life, to the marketplace, so to speak—after some days, weeks, or months—no matter what I do, clouds of mind reappear and the veiling stream of thought again takes control of my existence. Sir, the ego . . . it's dead, but it won't lie down!"

Raman smiled and seemed a bit straighter in his back this night. I noticed that he didn't invite the American up in the hot seat. "As you may know, I don't believe in the notion of 'killing the ego.' The result of such an approach mostly is an involuntary, subconscious strengthening of the same 'I, me, mine.' My approach is all about a shift in how you experience yourself, a recognition of your true consciousness-identity, and a corresponding rearranging of the house, the ego redeployed from the master-position to that of a useful servant. That being said, it is a most crucial theme for spiritual seekers that is here been raised by you. A taboo, almost. Because in the convenient mythology of Enlightenment, the search supposedly ends in one happily-ever-after blast of insight. A sellable fairy tale, but in reality it is for a minority that it happens as one final Awakening only and then the ego-trance is forever over and done with. For most, and this is not so often spoken about, the transcendence is experienced much more like two steps forward and one back, or, like you are sharing with us here, with an unknown number of non-lasting tastes of freedom."

Raman took a break, nodded to the American, and he nodded expectantly back.

"When freedom is near—the opposites, let's call them demons—are known to mobilize to pull you back. Back to mind-identity and conformity in the herd. Tests and testers appear. Fishing in your exterior as well as in your interior. And if you take the bait, another round of suffering and maya. Spiritually this has tentatively been explained as a result of karmic hindrances still operating in the seeker, psychologically, as results of unresolved issues and mind-generating holes in the psyche. Both attempts at explanation suggest some kind of purification as the solution. But more basic than this, I suggest that the main issue is that the bond with your personal identity is not yet broken. That also during an Awakening experience, it has been operating under the surface, just waiting for an opportunity to resurrect. As if the ego has reached its retirement, but still it keeps showing up for work."

The big American struck out his arms in obvious recognition. Raman gave him a reassuring smile. "So before we proceed, tell me: What practices have you done?"

"The last eight years, many. I have done two years of psychotherapy. And more groups than I can remember. Now I am practicing tai chi meditation and Self-inquiry."

Raman nodded, waited, and spoke. "In your case, from what I see, sense, and hear, don't worry too much. I say you are already over the hilltop."

The American looked perplexed. "What does that mean, exactly?"

"Apparently you have passed into what the Buddhists call the 'stream entry.' Meaning that you have had a taste of spiritual reality beyond any doubt and thereby have entered the 'stream' heading inevitably to the ocean of consciousness. Flowing downstream now. In your impatience you may not fully appreciate this, but it is worth celebrating, really. Progress from here will most likely seem to occur, sometimes faster and sometimes slower, but it isn't as much tied to one's sense of personal effort. Your sense of the path 'doing you' versus the other way around deepens from here on."

The American spontaneously bowed and Raman continued. "Tai chi, any heartfelt meditation, really, is fine. I also still enjoy a good meditation now and then. The noise of the outside world has a certain pull, and for me it is like cleaning the gathered dust off my innocence. Thoughts come and go, and this is not really the problem, but you falling into the trap of identifying with them is! Don't take the bait and get involved. If energy is not given, thoughts lose their pulling power, don't they?"

"Yes."

"So stay alert so that in the midst of the next storm, you don't forget your storm-sail, the key-inquiry-question: To whom does this 'veiling stream of thoughts' appear?"

"Consciousness of awareness."

"Also as you must know by now, about any Awakening experience, that 'reproducing it' cannot be forced. But what you can do, is to steadily inquire *who* is it that is interrupting it, *who* is reappearing and further *who* is holding on . . . ?"

"Yes, sir, I see your points. I do! Very clear, thank you. Who is holding on . . . Anything else, Raman? I am extremely thirsty."

New aspiring arms went up, but Raman took a break, considered the request, and closed his eyes. Then he smiled. "Who are you not? With 'stream entry' already on the table, are you familiar with the Buddhists' *contemplation of the six elements*?"

"No."

"Anybody? *Earth, water, fire, air, space,* and *consciousness*? Not familiar? Very well. Let's complete this evening with a guided meditation. Everybody find a good position. You may lie down if you like, or sit on the floor, but beware: Your mind might, under the cover-up of being bored, do its usual escape-number from an inconvenient truth, so I might hit you with my Zen stick if you allow it to drift you away! Okay? On the head!"

"Okay, Raman."

"Find your space, then, close your eyes, and wish your Self a good journey by repeating within: 'May I be well. May I be happy. May I be at peace . . .' Then fasten your seatbelts and be still."

From my lotus position with closed eyes, and with a tickling of expectation, I took three deep breaths and focused my attention solely on Raman's soft voice. I too wanted to be beyond doubt and step out in the stream entry.

"This never-outdated practice has its origin in the earliest written scriptures of Buddhism, the Pali Canon, where the Buddha paints his audience an understanding of existence consisting of six elements. So first let's summon what is called the Earth element externally. Imagine flying, looking out of the plane window and down. Seeing buildings, vehicles, roads, mountains, rocks, trees, and crops growing in fields . . .

"Having reflected like this on the Earth element externally, everything that is *solid and resistant* outside of ourselves, ending with the floor upon which we sit, or lie, we now call to awareness the Earth element within ourselves, everything solid that gives us form. Be aware of the flesh, sinews, bones, bone marrow, kidneys, heart, liver, diaphragm, and every other conceivable solid matter in the body, including the brain . . . You normally think of your form, your body, as being 'me,' as being myself, but now

I challenge you to recollect how everything of the Earth element that is within you comes from outside and returns to the outside. How your body and my body started with the creation of one cell from the fusion of a sperm and an egg from our parents, who are not me. The fertilized ovum divided and grew into an embryo as it absorbed nutrients from the world outside, from your mother's bloodstream, but ultimately from the plants and animals she ate. And from that point on in your life, every molecule that has contributed to the Earth element in this body, which you have been thinking of as 'me,' similarly has come from outside . . .

"The Earth element you experience in your body is all built up from the food you have eaten. There's not a single molecule of solid matter within this body that is self-originated. It's all borrowed. And you have to give it back. In fact you constantly are giving it back, every moment of your lives. The Earth element within you is constantly returning to the outside world. Solid matter is combusting within the body and being exhaled. Even your bones, which you may think of as the most solid and enduring part of the body, are involved in a never-ending process of being dissolved and rebuilt. Even your bones are processes rather than things. Materializing and dematerializing. Flowing through you like a river. The human body lives because it is a complex of motions, of circulation, of respiration, and of digestion. And as you recollect the Earth element flowing through you in this way, you can reflect: 'This is not me, not mine, I am not this. How can I claim to possess it, identify with it? How can I cling to something that's *panta rei*—all flowing?'

"So now you call to awareness the Water element outside of yourselves. The plane beams through a storm. Showers of water hit the fuselage. We dive under the clouds and see creeks and lakes. Rivers. The ocean, covering three-fifths of Mother Terra . . . Then you contemplate the Water element within our body—all that which is liquid, more than 60 percent. Starting with those manifestations that you can directly experience. Feeling saliva in the mouth, mucus, the pulse of the blood, sweat, the feeling of moisture in the out-breath, the pressure of urine in the bladder. Then you move on to those things you can only experience more imaginatively: lymph, fat, synovial fluid, cerebrospinal fluid, and all the liquid that permeates and surrounds every cell in the body including your brain . . .

"Then we recognize that all of the Water within the body, which you think of as 'me' and 'mine,' is in reality simply borrowed for a while from the outside world, that it's quite literally flowing through you, and that there is no single particle of Water element that is with you throughout your lives. How can you call something that is almost two-thirds floating water, temporarily borrowed from the outside, for 'me'? And so you reflect: 'This is not me. This is not mine. I am not this.'

"The Fire element outside is the raw physical energy in the universe, that which keeps the plane's jet engines running. Or more precisely, that energy deriving from the nuclear fusion in the heart of the sun and ending as habitual temperature in our planet's air and the energy stored in oil and in our food as fat, sugars, and proteins. Within us this warmth is metabolism. It's our energy. So in this meditative journey we can experience the heat of the body. Feel the cooler air we breathe in contrast with the warmer out-breath as it leaves the body. Feel the heart pumping and call to mind the myriad chemical combustions taking place at the cellular level; sparks of impulses in the muscles, nerves, and brain . . .

"All of this energy is borrowed from the Fire element outside of us. We feed the body by taking in the sun's light and energy embodied in plants or flesh. We warm ourselves in the rays of the sun, either directly or through burning fossil fuels that grew in the sunlight of ages past. And we have to keep replenishing the body's fuel because the element Fire is forever leaving: radiating from our skin, wafting away on our exhaled air, lost in the warmth of our feces and urine. We are totally dependent on the right amount of Fire element; too hot or too cold and we die. And so the Fire element, like Earth and Water, simply flows through us, unstoppable. And as we observe the energy within the body, we can be aware that it's actually another river—a river of energy—passing through this form, that it is really not ours at all. 'This is not me. This is not mine. I am not this.'

"Calling to awareness, then, the Air element outside of you, this atmosphere which envelops the whole earth and surrounds our imaginary plane, a floating air-submarine. The winds and clouds and breezes that you see and hear daily moving waves, branches, and grasses. The air surrounding you and touching the skin's pores in this very moment . . .

"Simultaneously recalling the Air element within the body. The air in our lungs and other body cavities, even the gases dissolved in your blood; you're immediately aware of the breathing, aware that air is flowing rhythmically in and out of the body . . . We all 'swim' in the same gas and breathe in the same air, and there's no boundary between inner Air and outer Air. There is only one Air element, and what's within you is simply borrowed for a few moments. You can't hold onto the Air element any more than you can hold onto any of the other elements. In fact you can only live by letting go, never by holding on. To hold on is to die. And so you reflect that 'the Air element, like the other physical elements, is not me, not mine, that I am not this.'

"You can't see the Space element, as it's not matter. You can't touch it and you can't say how far it extends. You can't even say what, if anything, it's made of.

The most you can do, for instance on a night flight, is looking out of the plane window and up to the starry sky and imagining all the space containing the stars. According to Einstein, this space expands and contracts, and this being graspable to you or not, as you're sitting or lying here with your eyes closed, you can try to feel what the first four elements—Earth, Water, Fire, and Air—within you occupy. But even when this form labeled your name is absolutely still, it is moving. The planet is spinning on its axis and revolving around the sun, the whole solar system is swinging around the galactic core, and the galaxy itself is rushing away from every other galaxy at an incomprehensible velocity. So although you might think there's a 'me space,' scientifically you're never actually in the same space for two consecutive moments. Space isn't really dividable into 'me space' and 'not-me space.' It's all one space, we are in it, it is in us, and it flows through us. As with the previous elements, it is borrowed. Space can't be owned.

"Ladies and gentlemen, we are now preparing for landing. If you have paid attention during this little flight and not escaped into a defense-trance, it must be impossible now not to realize that there is nothing to grasp on to, zero manifest that 'you are.' Our common awareness of this impermanence naturally then can turn its attention to itself. To that which perceives and realizes this, that dimension within that is deeper than thought, that which the Buddha introduced as the final element: 'Then there remains only the element of *consciousness*, bright and purified.'

"So within your combination of flowing elements, your form—demonstrably not who you in your essence are—sensations, thoughts, images, and emotions come into being, persist for a while, and then vanish into emptiness. Freed now of the bondage of being some *thing*, the insight of conscious living like this is realizing that all experience is simply passing through us in the same way that the Earth, Water, Fire, Air, and Space elements are flowing through our physical form. As our old friend Heraclitus put it: 'There is nothing permanent except change.' Change, and, never again to forget, that which are witnessing or observing this change, *consciousness*.

"Slowly come back, then. Return to here. Loosen your seatbelts and softly open your eyes."

A spirit odyssey with Captain Ram. Looking around a long moment, it was as if I had never seen the Satsang room before.

"Okay, Jennifer?"

"Okay, Raman."

"You have not yet awakened after so many years solely because you have succeeded so well in avoiding it!"

Spiritual Arrogance

"To know the truth of one's Self as the sole Reality, and to merge and become one with it, is the only true Realization." In my heart, and as an antidote to doubt, I carried this Ramana Maharshi quote back with me from a five days' motorbike pilgrimage northeast to the holy mountain of Arunachala. Walking in the footsteps of the last century's most renowned sage, meditating in his caves, and visiting the ashram he left behind. All in all an inspiring time out, but not my next step, I had decided, speeding back down the hills to Kerala between rains. I felt more alien to this variant of monastic life than I had expected; I longed only stronger for the ocean and for Captain Ram.

The sound of nature's invincible powers, of monsoon-rain pouring dramatically against the Kavalam-windows. And music. The sitar player was back. Tuning into the waiting silence, there was something . . . an unexplainable premonition inside of me of something extraordinary about to take place. As Raman was being wheeled to his place, I opened my eyes and again saw more people than last week. At least six people were already raising their hands, including . . . Silvia! She was late, but back. She hadn't, as I had been thinking, left Alappuzha. Now she was sitting in the back row with her hand in the air.

Raman remained as usual undisturbed by all this eagerness, ignored it even, and picked up something from his pocket instead, a letter. "I get an increasing amount of letters from all over the world. Though written words do not have the same potential of transmutation as being in presence together, I answer them to the best of my ability. This particular letter I received only yesterday, and I like to read it out loud. It is from one Richard in Canada: '*Beloved sir. My mind is terrorizing me. It is like a war zone in my head with no ceasefire, and controlling it is like walking my two dogs when one is in heat and trying to keep them apart. If you can send me instructions of how to stop this madness I will, if this is the proper way, wire you a nice bit of money.*'"

Raman laughed. "It sounds as if Richard wants to shop Enlightenment in the mail, doesn't it! Charmingly bold, but even if it was in my power to stop his mind via air-mail I certainly wouldn't do it. Why not? Firstly, because without any sort of preparing the ground, the stopping wouldn't last for long. Secondly because the jump-shift, due to the same lack of preparation, could simply be too gross to handle. The mental kickback may—rarely, but it is known to have happened—end up in a transient psychosis."

Raman read on: " *'It has reached a point where keeping a job is getting more and more difficult 'cause only when I am hiking and tenting in nature can I sleep well.'*"

Raman nodded. "Insomnia is a terrible disease. According to research an estimated more than thirty percent of the Western population are affected and ten percent have chronic insomnia. Consider these numbers. All, no doubt, due to a mind-activity that won't come to rest . . ."

He finished reading the letter: " *'I have tried therapy and hypnosis. And also several forms of meditation techniques, but I only experienced those as restlessness provocations, a sort of physical and mental self-torture. Excuse my ignorance, but I am desperate here. Please can you help me? Richard Harrington.'*"

Raman looked up from the letter and out to his listeners. "Lack of sleep is so life-reducing, isn't it? And in the West it deeply affects approximately more than 100 million people. Imagine such mental suffering, and Richard humbly prays for help. So how would you support him?"

Nobody moved. "Anybody? Yes, Silvia?"

Silvia smiled. "Somehow, meditation is still the answer."

Raman silently allowed this answer to sink in. Then he picked up another letter. "These are the words I replied to him this morning: 'Dear Richard, About ignorance and Peace, only those who don't know that they don't know are the truly ignorant.'"

He threw a glance at Silvia before he continued. "'*In your letter I sense a dawning awareness, a witness to your mental noise, so keep alert and make this observer your sanctuary. It is not within my role to advise you on any short-term aspects of sleep hygiene. This I believe you can look up yourself in the Internet. So even though I have no quick fix to offer, I do like to point out that meditation need not be something straining or separate from life. The best meditation often is found in putting your full attention into whatever are your everyday practicalities. So I suggest you practise it as if you are centered inside an invisible tent, and on the outside there is all kinds of turmoil: projections, memories, fantasies, and anticipations. Nothing which-is. Past-future thoughts. Or, for the sake of the hiking metaphor: unsolicited weather. So in washing your floor, cleaning your kitchen, driving your car, shopping for groceries, walking the dogs, or gardening your flowers, stay as present as you can and you will, a little by little, feel a spacious rest. And when your sharpened awareness catches the reluctant mind wandering off outside to noise and un-reality, away from the here-now, bring it with loving resolve, like a parent to a child, back home. Back to what is being done in the sanctuary of your peaceful tent—to the space of the moment. Through your letter I can sense your suffering, Richard, but don't despair, because even the wildest horse can be tamed, and if your steadfastness is strong enough, one sleepy night the battle will be won.'"*

Raman folded the letter, put it back in his pocket, and attached his eyes on Silvia. He nodded. "So much for long-distance communion. Such a gift to be here, rather, tuning in with the Self, isn't it? Come up here, Silvia."

Silvia eagerly found the seat and I felt a quiver of excitement. Without knowing it, I had been waiting for this moment. They looked at each other. Both smiling, none with any sign of anything to be said. Yet, after a gaze lasting a minute or so, Silvia eventually broke the silence. Knowing her, I say she spoke those first words in honesty, yet with a well-hidden undertone. Something like Edie Brickell's *I know what I know, if you know what I mean . . .* "There is no question, Raman, yet I guess meditation is still the answer."

"Absolutely not."

"But you just said . . ."

"The medicine prescribed to one being doesn't necessarily apply to another." Raman shook his head. "And too much medicine is known to be poison, so, quite on the contrary, to you, Silvia, I say the opposite: Stop all your meditation practices. Immediately!"

Silvia looked rather shocked at Raman. "Stop? But in all my years, with Suresha and others . . ."

"Yes, yes. You have been with Suresha for . . . ?"

"Six and a half years. And a lot of spiritual practice before and during that."

Raman took a long break and examined her thoroughly with his wide open eyes. "How come, then, Silvia, your final Realization has yet not happened?"

"My feeling exactly, sir. It simply seems that Suresha was not my final teacher, not my Satguru . . ."

"So if anybody is to blame, it is Suresha, but I know her as such a fine teacher?"

"No one is to blame. It is just what-is."

"Yes . . . and if I ask what you really want, the answer will be . . . ?"

"Peace in mind."

"All by the book."

"Yes . . . ?"

"Like 'Only if it's the will of the source.' 'Going with the flow,' 'All is one,' etcetera, etcetera."

Silvia looked confused. "What do you mean?"

Raman awaited, as if making an overall resolution. He then continued with an imperceptible sound of metal in the otherwise so soft voice. "Some teachers don't address this issue, maybe because they enjoy a court of advanced hang-arounds, but I cannot tolerate it. I simply care too much for this kind of dead-end suffering."

"I am suffering, sir?"

"Underneath it all, yes, Silvia. You see there is a great danger occurring for everybody cruising around in the spiritual circles year after year in that they are adapting a whole new set of conditionings, a makeup of 'me the seeker.' The one who seemingly through knowing all the concepts has reached further up the ladder than her fellow-beings, maybe even to a 'higher Self.'"

Silvia looked puzzled at him and involuntarily folded her arms. Raman observed and smiled. "Protectiveness. You see, Silvia, more and more is allowed invested like this in a subconscious urge to protect this, your superior spiritual story from . . . from the fear of that very which you are searching for. From the fear of a bottomless void of Reality, or let's say: nobody-ness."

"I am not afraid."

Raman paused again. "Yet, Silvia, it is my firm observation as a teacher, and my suggestion also for this here little dialogue of inquiry, that you have not yet awakened after so many years solely because you have succeeded so well in avoiding it!"

Silvia was about to fall off the hot seat. "Raman! This is a joke, for sure. There is nothing more I want in life than a profound Awakening!"

"Who wants an Awakening?"

"I knew you were going to say that. My . . . soul!"

"Then you also know my next question. Who knew what I was going to say?"

Silvia swallowed and tried to be still, but meeting Raman's open gaze, her own eyes were flickering and some automatic words slipped out through her dry lips. "A higher Self."

"Spoken with a small s, which is, higher or lower, as you already know, nothing but a labelled thought. What is the source of this thought? Can you find it?"

Silvia struggled. I could literally see her mind-activity and Raman didn't give her more space. He firmly proceeded. "So for the sake of this investigation and for the benefit of all, tell me honestly how Silvia wished her Enlightenment to happen?"

She was on guard now. "If, and how, it is all up to the source . . ."

"Again, so correct. Yet nobody has ever impressed their way into durable freedom, divinity, love, joy, or peace in mind, have they, Silvia?" Silvia didn't answer. "And now you know that I could ask: 'Who is trying to impress?' So I am going to let that go and rather state this to all of you: In the world of modern spirituality, in which Silvia is a veteran, it is overflowing with more or less grandiose stories of Awakenings. And I know that many of you secretly are feeding fantasies about the story one day to be told of 'me, the chosen one, and my divine encounter.' So, Silvia, would you settle for instance with Awakening as you were flushing the toilet after a third day of having a Mumbai surprise?"

Silvia looked angrily at Raman. "Why are you asking me these kinds of questions?"

"Because freedom cannot be controlled, Silvia. And it is my qualified suspicion that you—meaning your ego-mind—are trying to be the director of your own process. The one who did it and got it!"

"I am not the doer . . ."

"Then who are you?"

"Consciousness . . ."

"Again and again, the right word spoken, and once more without ingenuous gravitas. 'Those who know cannot say, and those who say don't know,' as the Kabir quote goes."

"The witness, then . . ."

Raman smilingly shook his head. "I hear the words, but they are not what I see in the mirror of your soul, in your eyes. Can't you by now, with your well-trained awareness, see the operating of a doer with an ongoing desire some day to celebrate her merits as a reputed writer, teacher, or guru? Because the film script of '*Me and my Great Awakening*—starring Silvia' is already written, isn't it?"

I had never experienced Raman so rough, so brutal, even, and my empathy mechanically moved toward Silvia as she straightened up in the hot seat. "Whatever you say, Raman. But I am the witness of this, not this doer!"

"And isn't it that this same director in your subconscious brought you here to Alappuzha so you could awaken more glittering, 'one level up,' by the teacher of your teacher?"

Silvia was dumb. Raman continued the interrogation just as pristine. "A director, or displaced controller, operating in aversion of losing her shaky safety and long-polished spiritual identity? Camouflaged as a higher version of 'me' and substituting the obvious lack of ability to undo herself by burying in words and practices of dharma, in pretty lotus flowers?"

Silvia was speechlessly out of character. As many probably would have stood up and left, Silvia, at least so far, heroically stayed seated. My sympathy despite it becoming thrillingly clear to me that I was witnessing somewhat of an enlightened character assassination.

"No reason to take it personally, Silvia, because you are perfectly right in saying that this is not You! Conditioned mind at play only. And I am putting this on the plate and under the Satsang spotlight, not to be mean, but in sincere compassion. Because I know too well that you can go on the rest of this lifetime 'being almost home' and laying stroke after stroke of spiritual makeup on top of a 'freedom' you will be left only fantasizing about. It's like hanging out in exotic restaurants, learning the menu by heart, but never getting to taste the food! And with an initial genuine thirst for truth, this is suffering. Self-betrayal and suffering."

Silvia swallowed. "Harsh words, Raman. A Zen stroke, excuse me for knowing. And if you are right, the treatment being . . . ?"

"First let's clarify what's in your way." Raman looked out on the crowd. "Regardless of this ongoing rainstorm, the sun is always there, isn't it? But just as clouds seemingly hide it, some subtle set of I- or me-thoughts hides Silvia's Self."

He turned his attention back to Silvia. "Ego-enchantment, regardless of costume, is an aspect of arrogance. So I suggest naming the, until this moment, unspotted cloud obscuring your sun a spiritual arrogance, upheld by a deeper unmet fear of losing control."

To her best ability Silvia took the diagnosis in, thinking, considering, and . . . protesting. "But how should this be possible? When I absolutely don't feel any fear!"

"I believe you, yet that doesn't mean it is not there. An invincible impulse, a fear of fear, and pop: Your conditioned mind is, in a split-second, ready in the form of defending and distracting thoughts to camouflage it."

Silvia shook her head in resignation. "Fear of fear . . ."

"Yes, but let's begin the treatment in the other end, rather. At the issue of arrogance and its opposite and antidote, humbleness . . . and also openness and gratitude. How do these key spiritual values blossom in our beings? Not by the ego-mind's effort, for sure. Quite the contrary. Rather, in experiencing its limitations in some rough encounters with outside circumstances. Or as the Buddha replied to a student who wanted to know why Enlightenment hadn't yet happened to him: 'Maybe you haven't suffered enough . . .'"

Silvia couldn't restrain herself anymore. She loudly objected. "Suffer more!? And meet a fear that I don't feel? I feel you're bullying me and waving in the dark, and I don't get it!"

"Start from there, then: in not getting it!" Silvia bit her tongue, as Raman made a long, silent pause. "Don't forget, Silvia, an obscuration cannot in any way be treated before it is seen and admitted by its beholder. So I am pointing out that beneath your surface, so well-dressed, spiritual ego-appearance, there is a fear of the fear of the unknown, of the Self itself, running your show."

Silvia looked more than unhappy, close to crying, even. And shivering. Suddenly what I had been fearing and waiting for happened. Determined, she got up to go.

"We are not finished, sit!" Raman's voice was like a whiplash. An impossible sound, really, coming from such a shrunken old body. Surprised, Silvia reluctantly sat down again and Raman continued with a ruthless flow of words.

"I am trying to shake you all out of your comfort zone here, because this matter one way or another will apply to you all now, or later, after my departure, so pay attention. On the freedom-journey, extra problems crop up when an identity crisis occur in a student out of her spiritual practice. Before you know it you may find yourself waxing and refining, and after years of investment it is almost impossible to let go, because subconsciously there is so much invested, so much to defend. To keep this attractive persona up, an intricate web of self-deceptions and subtle escape-strategies to avoid true seeing is developed. Not only is there then a me and my more or less beautiful relations, me and my high-grade career, me and my unproblematic past and my promising future, but on top this amazing cake is decorated with shiny candles: 'the spiritual me' celebrating itself. A seemingly pious character, in reality in a denial of all the underlying layers of distractions in the mind. This is the mask to mask all masks and an ultimate veiling of your true essence. A self-induced trance of not only identifying as a physical, mental and emotional body, but with an esoteric glaze overlaying everything. Still apparently searching for truth, but with a filter of automatic Satsang attitudes like: 'Yes, beautiful words, and *I* know them by heart already,' or 'The further *I* re-create myself in God's image, the more worthy of infinite divinity *I* get,' and 'One day *I* too will wake up, not now, not here, and not like this, rather more like the Buddha under the Bodhi-tree'"!

Raman laughed loudly at his own outburst. "Mind-deception at its best showing. It's a joke, isn't it?"

Silvia didn't laugh. She shook her head angrily. Suddenly she started crying. "What are you saying to me, Raman? What have I done? Should I stop being your student, maybe? Are you disqualifying me from Satsang?"

Raman remained unconcerned by her tears. "Consider the old metaphor, Silvia, of the finger pointing to the moon. The finger being the teaching and the moon Self-realization. If you, in all your searching, in your case for ten years or so, look solely at the details of the finger, you miss the moon entirely, don't you? A true teaching is nothing to be believed in or learned. It must be experienced, or better, realized, and then you can flush all the pretty rehearsed words together with a Mumbai surprise down the toilet!"

" 'Return to innocence,' then, as Suresha said . . ."

Raman shook his head. "Once again you are parroting concepts to keep your mind running and protected. This is your mind's way of settling for security and relative comfort! If I suggest to you a listening approach of not getting it, not-knowing, your mind almost with the speed of light responds: 'Yes, this I know! Return to innocence.' "

"Sorry . . ."

"Who's sorry?"

Silvia stayed silent. Her shoulders shivered. Like the bull in the bullfight, exhausted, with the horns lowered, having reached *momento del a veridad*—the moment of truth. There was a long break of silence. Silvia shivered again.

Raman nodded. "That's right, your ego is being humbled. Stay with it and toss all your self-importance on the fire. Satsang is just that: throwing all concepts, beliefs, and intentions on the flames of truth and nakedly witnessing the illusions burn!"

Silvia took a deep breath, and one more. She was struggling and shivering, struggling to keep quiet. And just as she was unable to remain inactive, Raman continued, with a voice slightly softer. "Very good, Silvia. Now give me some feedback. What's going on?"

After a long pause, Silvia whispered something, but I couldn't hear what she was saying, only see that Raman smiled. "With any fear there is an impulse to contract, and such mental habits die hard, but the fear-fueled ghost bugging your presence has been exposed, hasn't it?"

We all waited in breathless excitement, and then Silvia nodded imperceptibly.

"And with this exposure a glimpse is revealed of what is all I am talking about. Right, Silvia?" Raman looked lovingly at her. Fearfully, or delicately vulnerable, rather, Silvia's eyes flickered, and after some long seconds she nodded once again. Raman kept smiling. "Good. Your blind spots more than anything pull you down. So with my best intentions Silvia, mirroring you, allow me one final cut: In 'this Silvia' I see so many impressing identities operating. Born Jewish into 'God's chosen tribe,' maybe the best-looking female in Satsang, the one with the strongest Satori reports, as I have been told, on a scholar level the smartest or best 'studied' student, maybe, and doing chi qong meditation, even, and not to forget, yoga-mastery . . . How on earth do you think you can carry all this stuff with you through the infamous 'needle's eye'?"

Silvia seemed completely punctured as Raman kept finishing with his surgery. "There is an ancient story about a depressed rich man who sold all his belongings and travelled around the world with his gold in a sack in the pursuit of peace and contentment. He finally heard of a sage living in a small hut on the top of the hill. As he reached this destination, he dropped the sack of gold at the sage's feet and stated: 'All this is yours if you can bring back the happiness I remember from my long-lost childhood. Can you help me?' The sage nodded: 'But only if you follow my instruction.' The old man agreed: 'Where do I start?' 'You start by dropping your sack of gold in the river . . .' So, Silvia. Do you think he could do it?"

Silvia hesitated. "Drop my attachments . . . to my attainments?"

"At this point they are just massaging your ego, aren't they? Why do you think 'your' glimpses of Self remained just impermanent happenings? Isn't it maybe because a 'me' has been lurking in the shadows ready to at any moment jump out, spinning a story around it, reducing it to an experience, and claiming it as 'mine'?

Silvia met Raman's eyes for the first time in many minutes. "I have been pondering about that. Thank you, Raman."

"Okay, Silvia."

A sigh of relief went through the assembly. Impossible as it had seemed, a happy ending was about to unfold, but suddenly Silvia didn't want to leave. "And the further medicine being . . . ? Please, while I am under the knife and cut open on the operation-table, all seems wrong and there is nothing I can do . . ."

Raman giggled. "You cannot do being! Nonetheless there is plenty to be experienced and realized in staying true to that which initially got you started on this journey!"

"Right now I am not sure what that is anymore . . ."

"How about that which can be in awe just of the wonder of existence? *It* is near, Silvia, so meet whatever arises without moving. And when stillness happens, when Self reveals itself without any notions of what it should be like, let any appearing ghosts, fear, and thoughts just to pass through. Don't try to suppress anything, don't cling, and don't feed . . . Relax into the openness of not knowing. Allow *it* to be just thrillingly unknown and met without any strategies. This takes courage, Silvia, so go with that."

Silvia bowed her head. "Thank you, Raman, sat-guru."

"Very good. You can return to your seat, then."

As Silvia walked away, I tried to meet her eyes and show her my support, but she didn't look at anybody, didn't even sit down. Silvia just walked straight out of the Satsang room. Raman looked around at the remaining audience.

"Of this I am ever speaking it is first and foremost for the brave at heart. Such an exposure of mind and its seduction ability, wasn't it? So . . . in some cases, I may say a meditation practice is the right approach; in other cases, not. Inquiry, on the other hand: Inquire till there is no one left to inquire. Okay, everybody?"

"Okay, Raman."

"*Your life does have a purpose, so remain a light onto yourself . . . Spiritually speaking, we are all born as promises. You see to it that you don't remain just a seed.*"

Seeds No More

B ack from one of my little drive-abouts and close to
full presence. Young mister Shayamal, optimistically
waiting with his cricket bat under the arm, reluctantly
told me that a woman on a scooter had been by in the
backyard.

"What did she say?"

"Something about fruit . . ."

"Fruit?"

"Forbidden fruit."

A spiritual regression, I was sure, but I couldn't help it,
my inner space was all of a sudden reoccupied. Reduced
to a fruit platter? *Did I disappoint you? Or leave a bad
taste in your mouth? You act like you never had love. And
you want me to go without.* U2: "One." Or two—and an
involuntary stream of thoughts. What if I was at the brink
of a breakthrough, a let-go, and in the last moment now
failing the test and just escaping into fantasizing about
togetherness? *Avoiding the freedom-unknown, as Raman
had pointed out?* Yes, but what if all this newly acquired
rhetoric—aloneness-not-loneliness—was just a makeup

in my inner dialogue to cover up for some suppressed wounds and a fear of relating? *Then what, and what if? She had just been here trying to look me up; that must count for something?*

What if, and only one way to find out. Even though I had no idea where in Alappuzha she lived. Driving around the town it was like a repeating commercial. *A film scene, showing maple syrup skin, curved breasts, and stiff nipples, camera tilting down saying come, come, come . . . Self-hypnosis.*

The week passed. I ran across Silvia once. Random, in the middle of the rush traffic, in the opposite direction. She was on a scooter this time, with her hair easily recognizable under the scooter helmet, and she didn't see me. I was on my Royal Enfield, struggling to turn around, to follow her. A proper chase two blocks down, three to the left, and one to the right. Girl departed.

———◆◆———

Not a single square foot free. It was a full house. The Satsang room was packed with all kinds of nationalities. Two-thirds, probably, of whom were standing. The air was already thick and I couldn't spot Silvia's hair anywhere. The sitar music stopped as Raman was pushed into the room in his wheelchair by his wife Prathiba. It never used to happen; a nurse always did this job, and his wife never attended Satsang, but this evening she even stayed to listen. She sat close by her husband with a poorly concealed anxiety in her eyes. He waved away all her concerns with his cane, but physically he was so weak that he could barely speak.

"We will have just a short meeting. Why don't you ask something . . . a proper Satsang question?"

The room counted at least seventy souls, I gathered. All too shocked by the circumstances of their teacher to speak. Except for Mariana, who did her best to ease the situation. "Raman, beloved, tell us something about the essential. What is Enlightenment?"

"What is it? As you must know by now, Mariana, talking about it, conceptualizing it, lessens it. Words don't do it justice. There really is no language . . . no metaphors . . ."

Someone followed Mariana's lead: "Please, sir? I wish to know what I am thirsting for."

"So you are thirsting, are you?" Raman grimaced. "You sure know how to spark me off." He straightened up a little in the wheelchair, building movement, so to say. "*It is* . . . an indescribable joy . . . and a profound and undisturbed peace. And before I continue with more poor words, let it be said that there may be with the transitions into Self-realization as with snowflakes, no two being exactly alike."

"Tell us anyhow, about your own experience, how *it* came to you?"

Raman shook his head. "Okay . . . Just after my early pilot-retirement, some thirty-four years ago. After many years I had quit going to Satsang and was fed up with both searching and spiritual practice. Or so I thought . . . One spring morning, walking in my favorite park in New Delhi, in a flash and out of the blue, there was an incredible sense of sudden well-being, and as it happened, perception became shimmering bright, so to say, unclouded as it was by mind-activity. Grace was everywhere I turned. What I had considered normal for more than fifty years was no longer really normal, and the weeks to come brought quite an adjustment, a shaky upgrade of the hard disk, you may say. First months thereafter, a stabilization was falling in place. Unity. Leaving me with one interest only: a compassion for all suffering and the desire that other souls should also appreciate this freedom that had realized itself in me."

"And how has it evolved, what happened later? Now, Raman? What is it like, conscious living?"

"The initial nirvana doesn't last, or rather, the bliss comes and goes. But, of more importance, over the years I have discovered that there is a clearer understanding that occurs and that it is ever deepening. And underneath everything, the closest words that come to summarizing a 'state' of total presence are: *peace in mind.* With the inner noise, the mental movie-making, evaporated and gone. A spacious clarity where all the polluting thought-processes related to past and future are out of the way. And the remaining mind, the present mind, now undisturbed and extremely efficient also with an access to a deeper dimension, to insight and wisdom."

Raman took another deep breath. "Conscious living is peace and love manifest within, and as you play your role in life, whether as a shoe-polisher or a teacher, it radiates to the outside. Your being in natural service of uplifting other souls." Raman stopped, like an engine stopping. He looked exhausted. And in pain. Prathiba rushed up and made a sign to her husband.

The whole room spoke in a unison farewell. "Thank you, Raman!"

Raman Kavalam smiled through obvious agony. "Not quite. I want to wrap it all up. Everybody! Your life does have a purpose, so be a light onto yourself . . . Spiritually speaking, we are all born as promises. You see to it that you don't remain just a seed. That you grow and that you reach your ultimate potential—your fragrant flowering—now, in this lifetime."

Prathiba loosened the brakes on the wheelchair. People from four continents gave way as she helped Raman abandon the room. The doors closed behind my teacher and the room was left in utter silence.

"You are the unchanging consciousness in which every physical and mental object is occurring. Not recognizing this is to suffer, realizing it is freedom."

Water in Motion

The Alappuzha River was not the Ganges, but the water flowed almost equally dirty. Dirty and, on this occasion, sacred. Several hundred people were gathered on the riverside. The little wooden boat, full of fire material, with Raman's dead body dressed in white and lying on a stretcher, was now ignited by Prathiba's flaming torch. Soon the flames licked around Raman's well-known and beloved form. Compared with my own culture's displacement, this was death met shockingly unfiltered. The blazing boat was pushed into the river stream. Tears flowed as Raman's burning remains disappeared from me.

Watching the burning boat depart, something Raman had said when I saw him for the first time came to mind. A fragment from the over-my-head debate with the philosophy professor from Jaipur. That, in his concept, the body, initially a sperm meeting an egg and subsequently food material, was nothing but dead meat without consciousness. Consciousness being *the true identity* which manifested itself in the moment of conception and returned home to the un-manifest, the Absolute, in the moment of death. A sudden bang stopped my mind. Five hundred yards down the river, the boat and its cremation fire suddenly exploded in a rainbow of colors, in fireworks! Raman Kavalam's last greeting, his last words.

Silvia had left Alappuzha, flying back to her teacher in Tel Aviv, only a few days before Raman's death and departure. Deliberately without encountering me, she had left me a purple farewell letter explaining that it was meant for her to meet me and through our encounter become conscious of her last little knots, a desire for Raman's certification, and her still-to-be-worked-on fear of letting go into the unknown. And despite all she had said, some harsh words which were mainly from envy, I should trust Raman's spotted interest in me. I didn't have her obstructive fear and she was sure that one day, like a true Bodhisattva, I would wake up many people. Finally, she didn't expect me to understand, but unfortunately, despite true feelings, there could never be any "us" because of the prohibitive fact that I was a *goyim*.

A goyim? Once again taking stock, my love-object would not recognize me because my mother was not of true blood, not of her tribe. And my first and only teacher had awakened a thirst in me that was not quenched before he left his body. Back in Oslo a possible six months' imprisonment was coming up. I had made a call and, according to the police, the longer I waited to return, the longer sentence I would get. On the other hand I was drug free, even the cigarettes were dropping off. And all of my tendencies toward suicidal thoughts, angst, and despair were nothing but a dusty memory. The DJ within was playing U2 again: *I still haven't found what I am looking for.*

Weeks later I was wandering up and down the unending Kerela Beach, hiking long hours along the waves, accompanied only by a black stray dog I had named Tiger. It felt as if there was nothing more to lose in life. And that no teacher was greater than nature. I knew that I myself was the only phenomenon in the way of *it* revealing itself. And that the only gateway was the space of the moment.

But I was pondering: *How quickly does mind create an image of what's experienced? Does the present ever exist for us? Or is it always a memory before we truly perceive it?* As weeks went by, in my single-pointed hermitage, the rushing sound and the carbonated waves evaporating on the hot sand had to be the answer. A sound and a sight that didn't give mind much space or time to hold on or to conceptualize the impression. A brief moment of non-labeling.

No watch, no calendar. No computer, TV, or radio. Tiger comes running up from the foaming waves with the stick playfully in his mouth. My beard is long. About

Awakening, I just don't care anymore. I throw the stick once more into the water. Tiger folds himself into the stormy sea. Suddenly, no longer drained by thinking, ignoring thoughts, I can feel it: "my" own presence! And in the same moment I fully understand the small letters of Raman's **Freedom from this "me"** flyer sparkling clear: "You are the unchanging consciousness in which every physical and mental object is occurring. Not recognizing this is to suffer, realizing it is freedom."

Day by day a tremendous well-being fills my wading steps. Waves dance about my ankles in the magical sunset reflection. Everywhere around, in the appearing space of the moment, are reflections of consciousness. I am. I am that I am. Intensely alive. Whether it is *the* lasting Enlightenment? I close my eyes, see no light, and smile. *Who* cares?

Bibliography

Amon, Nissim. *The Book of Dharma: A Collection of Buddhist Wisdom and Zen Secrets.* Paros, Greece: Taos, 2005.

Balsekar, Ramesh. *Advaita on Zen and Tao.* Mumbai: Yogi Impressions, 2008.

____. *The One in the Mirror.* Mumbai: Yogi Impressions, 2004

Gangaji. *The Diamond in your Pocket.* Boulder, CO: Sounds True, 2005.

____. *Freedom and Resolve: The Living Edge of Surrender.* Ashland, OR: Gangaji Foundation, 1999.

Ingram, Catherine. *Passionate Presence: Seven Qualities of Awakened Awareness.* Portland, OR: Diamond Books, 2008.

Jaxon-Bear, Eli. *Sudden Awakening into Direct Realization.* Tiburon, CA: New World Library, 2004.

Maharaj, Nisargadatta. *I Am That.* Durham, NC: Acorn Press, 1973.

Maharshi, Ramana. *The Essential Teachings of Ramana Maharshi.* Carlsbad, CA: Inner Directions, 2001.

____. *The Spiritual Teaching of Ramana Maharshi.* Boston: Shambala, 1988.

Mooji. *Breath of the Absolute.* Mumbai: Yogi Impressions, 2010.

_____. *Writing on Water.* London, England: Mooji Media, 2011.

Osho. *Seeds of Wisdom.* Pune, India: The Rebel Publishing House, 1981.

_____. *Sat-Chit-Anand.* Pune, India: The Rebel Publishing House, 1988.

Poonja, H. W. L. *The Truth Is.* York Beach, ME: Weiser Books, 2000.

Sangharakshita. *What Is the Dharma?* Birmingham, England: Windhorse Publications, 1998.

_____. *Who Is the Buddha?* Birmingham, England: Windhorse Publications, 1994.

Taylor, Steve. *Waking from Sleep: The Causes of Awakening Experiences and How to Make Them Permanent.* Carlsbad, CA: Hay House, 2010.

Thompson, Berthold Madhukar. *The Odyssey of Enlightenment: Rare Interviews with Enlightened Teachers of Our Time.* San Rafael, CA: Wisdom Editions, 2003.

Tolle, Eckhart. *Stillness Speaks.* London, England: New World Library, 2003.

_____. *Oneness with All Life.* New York: Penguin Group, 2008.

About the Author

Espen Vidar is the founder of Oslo Film and Television Academy. Besides teaching, scriptwriting, and consultancy, he has directed eight short films, one of which is an international prizewinner (*Down and Out*, main prize in Capalbio Cinema International Short Film Festival in Tuscany, Italy, 1996). A black moment, a depression, and a life crisis threw him off the "train of outer more" and catapulted him to India, to the initiation of an inward journey and to enlightened teachers in the East and in the West.

www.ingramcontent.com/pod-product-compliance
Lightning Source LLC
Chambersburg PA
CBHW030517260626
47157CB00005B/1775